FIGHTING FOR CHLOE

HARPER PHOENIX
EVA JONES

This book is a work of fiction. Names, characters, places, and incidents either are the product of the author's imagination or are used fictitiously, and any resemblance to actual persons, living or dead, business establishments, events, or locales is entirely coincidental.

All rights reserved.

No part of this book may be reproduced, scanned, or distributed in any printed or electronic form without permission. Please do not participate in or encourage piracy of copyrighted materials in violation of the author's rights. Purchase only authorized editions.

Fighting For Chloe
Copyright 2018, Harper Phoenix, Eva Jones

ACKNOWLEDGMENTS

Jeesh, where do we even start!?
We'd like to thank all of you who believed in our dream and helped us to achieve it, you know who you are! To the sassy ladies who keep us sane; Joz, Antonette, Stacey, Amali, Sienna, Laura- We love you hard!
Tania, Lesley, Amali, and Cheril- Thank you so much for being our alpha readers and making sure we stayed on track. To our beta and arc readers- Without you we couldn't have done this! You all rock!
Ginormous sized thanks go to Amali Rose for your unwavering support and kindness, for giving us honesty when needed and being our sounding board! You amaze us both!
Antonette Santillo... You're our rock! We love you forever and always. 'Nough said.
Thanks also go to JM Walker for designing the awesome cover and formatting our words so they can be read in all formats. And special thanks to Anna Bloom, our editor, for going on this journey with us and for putting up with the both of us, we love you!

Those we love never go away, even when they can't be physically present.
They walk beside us. Still loved, and still missed.
~ Anonymous ~

PROLOGUE

Dominic
Nine Years Old

I'VE GOT A new bike. It's all I wanted and I can't believe my nan actually got it for me. It's my birthday, I'm nine today. I ride my bike up and down the pavement, Nan told me when I'm here I can play in the street, between the two lamp posts at either end, so long as I don't go past either one, I'm good. We've come for tea, Mum never cooks like my nan does, so I always have seconds and a pudding. I'm allowed because she said I'm a growing lad. I am, you know. I'm on my second pair of school trousers already this year. Mum said if I grow anymore she's taking the hem down because she can't afford to keep up with me. My nan buys my uniform anyway, my mum and dad don't.

As I turn my BMX around, and loop my way back down the street, a group of bigger boys come around the corner. I know who it is straight away, so I try and peddle off, but my foot slips. The ringleader, Tommy, is the hardest in my school and he's horrible to everyone. As my shin scrapes against the peddle, I start to fall. Laughter rings out behind me and I know they are watching me. Before I can pick myself up he's in front of me, his friends close by, blocking me in. I start to shake and it makes me mad. I shouldn't show weakness. I know this, yet I can't stop it. My heart echoes in my head. I flinch when he lifts his arm, thinking he's going to punch me. Instead he fakes it, and slicks his hair back, laughing because I flinched. He pulls his leg back and kicks my bike.

'Don't you dare kick my new bike.' I yell at him surprising even myself.

'What you gonna do 'bout it?' He stamps aggressively on the front wheel, and I push my chest out and yell again.

'I'll tell my dad and he'll kick your head in.' He wouldn't. He wouldn't give a shit about me, or my bike. But I wasn't going to tell them that. Tommy turns to walk away and I start to pick up my bike. The wheel is buckled, and I hold back stinging tears, but when I turn my back, he pushes me over, and I fall onto my bike. The handlebar sticks me in the ribs and I scrape my face across the pavement. My eye is closing up, it hurts so bad. My heartbeat pounds louder and louder. Just as I'm getting up he kicks me right up the arse.

'Yer bike's shit,' he says. They all walk down to Tommy's house, on the corner of the next street. I can't ride my bike because the wheel's all bent out of shape, so I push it best as I can back to my nans. I cry all the way back. I've been desperate for this bike, for as long as I can remember, and my nan has saved up to give me it. Now I can't even ride it. I walk around the back of the house and stand it up against the wall, before I sit on the floor and pull against the wheel with my hands while I force my feet against the bottom. It won't straighten. I sit and cry with my head on my knees, my nan comes out to see what's up. Pulling my face towards hers she gasps in shock.

'What the hell happened, did you fall off the bike?' I shake my head and swallow the lump in my throat as I swipe at the tears running down my cheeks, proof that I'm weak. Boys don't cry.

'What the fuck happened?' Dad yells from the backdoor. Great. 'Answer me, boy.'

'It was Tommy, he pushed me over and broke my bike.'

'And you fucking let him?' My chin quivers and I nod in answer. 'Where does the little fucker live?' I shrug my shoulders. I know, but I also know what my dad's going to do. He isn't mad they've hurt me. He's mad that I let them. Now I'll be taught a lesson. It's always the same. Nan stands with her hands on her hips, before she takes my chin with her fingers to examine my face.

'Let's get you inside and clean up your face.' She smiles at me, but she's not happy, she's sad, I can tell.

'The fuck he's going inside, get your arse over there right now and you kick his arse, otherwise I'm going to kick yours all over this fucking street, you hear me, boy?' It takes a minute to understand what he's just said and I'm slow to stand. My nan starts to protest, but he ignores her, dragging me round the front of the house by my shoulder. He grips it so hard I know I'll have a bruise tomorrow. Nan's still calling us as we reach the front gate and I spot the lads hanging around outside of Tommy's house.

'You don't get respect by acting like a fucking little girl, Dominic. You *earn* respect, and you don't let cunts like them smack you around, you listening, boy?' I don't answer. When we get closer I can see Tommy straighten his back waiting for my dad to rip him a new one. He doesn't though.

'Which one of you cunts is Tommy?' he asks. None of them answer, so my dad turns to me. 'Which one?' I point at Tommy my face getting hotter and hotter. Tommy doesn't say a word. Just stands there looking dumb. My dad lets go of my shoulder and shoves me toward him.

'You sort this out like men do, you don't let anyone smack you around, Dominic. Now you fight him or I'll beat the fucking pair of you!' Tommy laughs like my dad is some kind of funny man. I know different. He's dead serious, and I have to decide what will be the lesser of two evils. Tommy fucking me up, or my dad. I make a quick decision and bring my hands up like the boxers do on the telly. My dad grunts in approval.

I go forward and Tommy sticks his hands up quickly realising what I'm doing. He's about twelve years old, and a lot bigger than me. I swing my arm out and land a punch just under his jaw. I aim for his face but hit his throat. He bends forward giving me an opportunity to punch him again. So I do. Twice more before he falls on his arse. Like I said he's a lot older than me, and a lot bigger. He surprises me by grabbing a handful of my hair, and then he rains punches into my stomach and chest. I've suddenly got no air and he still doesn't stop. My nose crunches and I feel warm liquid run down over my lips. He kicked my bike. He said it was shit. And now he's busted my nose. Bastard. I go wild and kick him in the shins. Hard. Then I punch him with both hands over and over until he finally lets go of my hair. He's bleeding now and is on his knees in front of me. Before I can do anymore damage, Tommy's dad comes barrelling down the road, headed in our direction.

'Don't stop, boy,' Dad orders. So I punch him again. He looks like he wants to give up now and I want to too. But as his dad gets to my dad, all hell breaks loose. There is screaming and cursing, and the next thing I know my dad is beating Tommy's, and my mum is out screaming at Tommy's mum that she will kick her arse to kingdom come. There's complete and utter chaos before the police are finally called and my dad is arrested. I learnt a lesson that day. And I never let anyone pick on me again.

Dom

I LOOK IN the shitty mirror and flex, I'm tatted up, broad as hell and fit as fuck. Have to be, where I come from it's the survival of the fittest. And I'm the fucking fittest.

No excuses.

No giving up.

In it to win it.

When I walk in the ring I'm there to do one thing. Take my opponent down. There's no rules, anything goes. No medic on standby to wheel you away when you get hurt. Best you can hope for is being dumped in an alley somewhere you might be found. Losing isn't an option for me. It's not just that, there's a big payday after each fight if you win. I need that money. So I take them out. It's me or them. It's my third fight in two weeks, I ache but it's a good ache. It keeps me on my toes and the pain is a reminder of why I'm here.

The place is a shit hole and I'm in what was once a public toilet, the sinks are fucked, the taps don't work, and I dread to think what the toilets are like. I wrap my knuckles in red wraps, it was a pain in my ass at first to do it on my own, trying to wrap my right hand with the left but I've learnt now. It was a case of having to. My knuckles have been broken and popped too many times to count. It's not much protection but it's better than nothing at all. I shake my arms and jump from foot to foot on the spot, cracking my neck from side to side. I put my mouth guard in and push the door open. The crowd are screaming for blood and I push my way through them. The fight before mine is over and the guy is being dragged from the cage unconscious. He's a mess. His first time, and no doubt his last. He's tossed to the side like fucking garbage. Paying him no more attention than I need to, I make my way up the stairs and into the cage. The little guy who announces the fighters is crudely mopping at blood with a white towel—it smears in arcs across the ring and his attempt to make it better fails. I step in and start to stretch my legs, side stepping around the cage. Arms shook out and rolling my neck some more until it clicks, I absorb the ache. Getting in the zone. I need to hurt this fucker and fast. I don't need to put my body through any more shit than necessary today. *In and out Dom.*

My opponent comes in the ring. I've seen him before and he's a good fighter. I've watched him take a few down, but he hasn't come across me yet. I won't be going down. Not for him. Not tonight. Not ever, if I can help it.

He's about my height maybe an inch or two taller. He isn't as broad as I am but he has the muscle. He stares at me from the opposite side of the cage. Trying to psych me out, not going to happen, just a walk in the park. I glare back curling my lip slightly. My eyes never leaving his. There's always a few minutes while all the greedy fuckers in the crowd exchange money for bets. Deciding on who they like for the win. I haven't lost a fight yet, but neither has this guy. He's about to though. I clench and unclench my fists, pacing back and forth in front of him. Eager to get this done. The little guy comes in and raises his arms, the crowd goes quiet. He doesn't say shit, we know the rules. Fight until you can't. That's it. He Yells out, 'To the left we have Dominic the Dominator, to the right, Jake the Jackhammer.' Fucking stupid names if you ask me but it gets the crowd going. I watch him waiting for the clap of his hands to signal the beginning of the fight. His hands meet but the echo is lost in the thunderous roar the crowd makes baying for blood. With one thing on my mind I step forward, paying no attention to the little guy running for freedom from the cage. My eyes are on the Jackhammer. He dances a little on his toes, spinning his fists like he's skipping a rope. I wait a beat of a second before I rush him not giving him time to protect his face as I fake a blow to the gut, with my right hand. I'm a righty, it's obvious for anyone to see in my stance, but I've learnt to use my left with just as much power. He hasn't done his homework like me. He doesn't see my left uppercut coming. It's that simple, that easy, he's out cold. One punch. Like I said, it's a walk in the park. The crowd goes wild, and I raise my left fist in appreciation. The little guy comes back in and he looks pissed. I grin.

'You bet on the other guy?' He shakes his head at me. 'Fuck Micky you should know better.' I grin harder and turn to leave the cage. As I hit the bottom step, I see a beautiful woman, her auburn hair drops below her shoulders in waves and her plump lips press into a hard line. It's hard to take my eyes off her. Of course, there are women here all the time, they often watch the fights and then try it on after, wanting a walk on the dark side with a bad boy fighter. I know the types. But this one, takes up all my attention. I stand a beat of a second too long and the guys trying to dump my opponent out of the ring grumble as I block their path.

Time is money here, and the next fighters are already on their way in. I move out of their way losing her in the crowd. *Fuck.* I have an urge to find her and I scan the crowd until I see her. One of the big guns has his hand wrapped around her upper arm, like he's forcing her to stay at his side. Her auburn hair is pristinely done. As if she feels my gaze, her eyes meet mine. My dick jerks in appreciation, and before I know what I'm doing, I work my way towards her. Before I catch up, she's being dragged away, I try to follow, but I lose them through a side door. It's guarded, and the guy shakes his head at me as I approach. I keep walking toward the door as if I didn't see the movement. His hand comes up to my chest.

'No entry,' he says in a strong gypsy accent.

'Come on man?' I plead.

'No fuckin' entry,' I know I could take this idiot down. But I also know that I won't like the consequences. So, I walk away. Pissed off. But, I can't afford to lose these paydays, certainly not over a fancy looking pussy. I make my way over to the cash desk and collect my earnings. A grand a fight is easy fucking money.

***

Chloe

My one opportunity to escape and I get distracted by a damn fight? What the hell is wrong with me? Okay maybe it wasn't specifically the fight, maybe it was more the man in the ring built like a tank who took the other guy as though he were nothing. The moment my eyes landed on him, everything else ceased to exist. As he left the ring our gazes locked and for a fleeting moment we just stared at each other. Could he have felt the same thing I had?

'Get the fuck in there!' A shove through the door I've just tried to run through, brings me back to the present. I chance a glance backward before I'm through the door and he's there, coming towards us. I didn't manage to get his attention, I should have been screaming for help but instead I was rendered speechless. I'm a moron.

'Why are you doing this to me? I already told you my father won't pay the ransom. He disowned me years ago.' I screech the last part, hoping they will get it through their thick skulls.

The douchebag henchman finally lets go of my arm and I start to pace back and forth in the shoebox sized office they have me holed up in. My father and I stopped seeing eye to eye years ago, when I was old enough to notice his career took the main focus in his life. I was nothing but an afterthought. All I ever wanted was to be a family and considering he was all I had left, I wanted that with him. So, when our relationship hit its final trial and nothing good came from it, I cut ties and bailed. Left the States and ran clear across the ocean to my favourite vacation spot. London. My mom used to bring me here and we'd spend all day looking at the sights and shopping. Dad never came with us.

'Chloe come sit down.' My main captor, Patrick, commands through gritted teeth, his American accent clanging against all the British sounds I've been around. He's sitting behind a beat up mahogany desk, his face is a furious mask. I do as he says and drop into the chair directly opposite of him. 'We're not going after your father for ransom money. If he hadn't stolen two million from us we wouldn't be in this position. I wouldn't have needed to send these two after you, to try to get my money back.' He points behind me to the two towering English goons who took me from outside my apartment this afternoon when I was getting home from work.

'Why would my dad have stolen money from you? The firm pays him a cushy little pay check. He's never had money issues.' I'm sure the confusion is written all over my face.

'Did you get a good look at where we're at princess?'

'Yeah, we're at a fight sitting in your crappy office.'

He laughs at my response. 'It's not a normal fight, princess. It's an underground fight and the only reason people attend is to place bets and watch people get beat to a pulp. I host these fights here and in the States. I met your father at one.' He waves a hand as if this is all boring. 'The details don't concern you anyway. But I want my two mil back and I will do what I need to get it. And right now, that means keeping you until the money's paid back.'

Patricks eyes are dark and dangerous. I know my dad used to dabble in gambling in his spare time when I was growing up. But this is all so much to take in. He may have been a shitty father but he did good business, or so I thought. How much has changed in the three years I've been gone?

'Well, as I said, my dad and I are no longer on speaking terms and it's been that way for some years now. I really don't think he's going to drop everything and rush over here to save his estranged daughter. Especially if he doesn't have the money to pay you back. You could just let me go and I won't report it to the authorities. This could all end now.' I chew on my lip nervously while waiting for him to respond. Patrick stands abruptly and makes his way to the door, pulling it open, as he leaves he turns back towards me—his parting words crystal clear.

'He will pay, or else.'

CHAPTER TWO

Dom

I HAVEN'T SLEPT well in days. Nan isn't well and I've been up with her through the night. Thank fuck for Zoe next door. If not for her I'd never be able to fight at the weekends. If I don't fight I can't pay nans mortgage. She shouldn't even have a mortgage at her age, no-one in their right mind would give her one, but somehow my deadbeat father, managed to swindle her. Whichever crook went along with him, convinced her to sign the fucking paperwork to re-mortgage her home for the next five years. Nan has no income other than her pension and the house was outright owned. Only way to get that debt paid off would be to sell, but all her memories are here, of my grandad and even my best childhood memories too. No. There is no way she's not living out her last days here. That's why I fight for money. It's a quick earner, and it means I'm around through the day for her.

Zoe thinks I'm working the door at various clubs, it's a good cover because of the times I leave for 'work'. She sits in with nan who's usually asleep, but it gives me peace of mind, and Zoe gets cash in hand and gets to watch Sky TV in return. I pay for that too because my nan loves the alibi channel. Always with the crime and murder solving shows. All from about two decades ago. But it keeps her happy with hours on hours of her favourites, so I pay the ridiculous bill every month regardless. I'm not beyond working a regular job and I'd do it in a snap if I didn't have nan to care for around the clock. Yeah, I could get a nurse in and whatever the authorities would sort for her home help, meals made and that sort of stuff. But it would be minimal and she'd be alone the majority of the time, and I can't live with that.

It's Friday night and fight night. My mind wanders again to the auburn-haired woman I saw last week... I've thought about her every day. And most definitely every night. She's been the last image in my head when sleep has finally taken me.

I've prepared for tonight. I've watched YouTube videos of my opponent and I know his tells, where he's weak and what I can do to take him out. So I'm quite relaxed as I wrap my hands in the shitty bathroom in the back. A commotion clamours on the other side of the door and I'm sure I hear a woman scream. I check to see what's going on and as I push the door open I get an eyeful of two brawny men in black suits. One of them is bent at the waist picking up a woman from the concrete floor. I take in the sight of her and quickly realise she's *the* woman. The one who's been playing on my mind for a week.

Without thinking, I move in front of the guy trying to haul her up off the floor, it's clear she doesn't want his hands on her.

'Hey,' I warn him. 'Leave her alone.'

'What's it to you, prick?' He puts his hands on me. That's his first mistake. His second is when he tries to pick the woman up from the floor again. Forcibly. No. That's not how you treat a woman. I cock my arm and punch him square in the jaw. He goes down without a problem. But we've attracted a crowd, it seems the fight in the cage isn't holding the crowd's attention anymore. As the second guy throws a punch, I duck and jab, hitting him twice consecutively in the solar plexus. He gasps for air and gives me the perfect opportunity to haul her up from the floor, and into my arms. She's bleeding from her nose and her face is all scraped up. Bastards. I walk us back into the toilets, but she panics.

'I need to get out of here, please help me, they're going to kill me—'

'Who is? What the hell is going on?'

'Please I need to get out of here now, before he finds out I'm gone.' She's slurring and her pupils are huge. She's fucking high. Great.

'He kidnapped me.'

'Who did?' But the hairs on the back of my neck stand on end and I have a bad feeling she's telling me the truth. When I saw her that first time she looked stunning, beautiful and fresh. That was a week ago. And she's still in the same clothes. Her hair is ragged and she has old makeup on her face. Fuck. What the hell have I got myself into?

Only seconds have passed and she's begging me to get her out. I grab my bag and pull out my hoodie, throwing it over her head and shoulders. I pull the hood up and over her hair and tell her to step into my joggers, like the hoodie they bury her. Trying to think quick, I unwrap my hand, and using it as a belt, wrap it around the top of the pants. It looks ridiculous and probably won't work for shit, but when I pull the hoodie back down over her waist, tucking it under a little to hide the length, she looks like she could almost pass for a teenager.

'You need to walk right out of this door and go to the entrance, you walk with me, don't look at anyone okay?' She nods at me, but I'm not convinced. I should just call the police, but then on the other hand I'm here, and this whole fucking place is illegal. I can't go to jail; my nan needs me.

'Listen to me okay, you want to get out of here, you do what I say? You understand?'

'Yes...yes...Please just let's go.' The desperation in her voice is clear despite the slurred speech. I push the door open and make my way to the front doors with her on my heel, still wearing my shorts and t-shirt. Luckily the fight in the cage has everyone's attention again, despite the two guys still knocked out by the door. I walk casually and as we get through the entrance I feel her physically stiffen as she grabs hold of my waistband. Her fingers are literally inside my shorts. I turn to check her out, to make sure she's doing okay, but in my peripheral, I see the reason for her alarm. We pass the guy she's scared of with ease just as the place erupts into cheers and applause. The fight must be coming to a close. Do I stay and fight or flee with her? If I go they will know I took her. As quick as the plan forms, I turn a corner and head for the main street, hailing a cab. I rummage in my bag and get my phone. I put her in the back seat and give the cabbie my address, handing him twenty quid.

'Straight there, and make sure she gets in safely, okay?'

'Sure, no problem,' he answers.

I turn to her. 'I'm going back in for my fight, that way they won't know you are with me, okay?' She nods but I don't think she's registering what I'm saying. 'I'll be back as soon as I can. I want you to stay inside once you get there.' She nods again. I have to accept it. I tap on the roof and the cabbie takes off. I run back down the side street and type out a quick text.

Me: Zoe a friend of mine is on her way. I've put her in a cab, please let her in and make her comfortable till I get home. Thanks.

Zoe: Sure no problem.

Me: Don't leave until I get home though.
Zoe: kk

The announcer calls my name just as I walk back through the door. I stash my stuff under the canvas and move up the stairs. I only have one wrap on my right hand. The other is around her waist. Fuck. I don't even know her name. I look over to the door of the bathroom; the guys are gone. I look over to the other door where I saw them take her last week. Two men stand guard, not the same two men, although they have the same suits and tics as the others. There's no doubt in my mind that they work for the big money who runs this operation.

My mind is not on the fight and I'm not prepared at all when my opponent swings and hits me square in the nose. *Fuck Dom get your damn head in the game.* I shake my head and clear the blur of fogginess caused by the right hook. I focus and dance as the guy moves.

I'm quick on my feet and have enough muscle to take down any man. This guy is a good fighter, against people who don't plan, and strategize. Against me, he has little chance of getting another lucky hit like that first one. It pisses me off he got that one. But it only makes me more determined to end this quickly. I don't want to waste any time but I also don't want to rush it. Rushing means mistakes. I can't afford mistakes, especially not tonight. I sidestep as he goes in to swipe my legs. He catches the shin on my right leg instead of the back of my calves like he intended. It hurts, but the look on his face as the small bones in his foot connect with my shin bone, tells me it hurt him a fuck load more than it did me. I smile. My eyes are wide and I grin as I move in to take him down. I jab to the solar plexus, ribs and kidneys, as I dance around him, repeating it twice. As the second kidney punch connects, his breath rushes from his lungs and he lands on his knees. His hands go out to stop him face planting the canvas. Normally I would wait until he's back on his feet. But I have no time for that shit, I need to be gone. A punch to the temple. And he's out. I'm done. I don't celebrate. I just make my way to the cage door and move to grab my stuff, the announcer throws all sorts of praise my way, but I'm already moving to the desk to get my winnings. It's as I wait for my money I spot the two goons I knocked out earlier. Great. One stands either side of the desk. The money man is counting out my payroll and hands me my money. I thank him and turn to leave. But the two guys flank me on either side and steer me toward the door I wasn't allowed through before. On the other side is a small office a big desk and an older guy behind it.

'Dominic the dominator!'

I frown. 'That's the circus name, name's Dom.' I stretch my hand out for him to shake and he takes it.

'You're a good fighter.'

'I like to get paid,' I answer abruptly. 'Listen I have places I need to be, what can I do for you?' We need to get to the fucking point.

'Well it's funny you should talk about getting paid, it's something we both have in common. You see if I don't get paid, I get pissed and when I'm pissed there's never a good outcome. Usually I don't have any problems getting paid. But…and it's a big but, there was one exception. I was ripped off and I don't take kindly to that, Dominic, not kindly at all.'

I frown at him in question. 'What the fuck has that got to do with me? Sure as shit I didn't steal your money.'

'No, quite right, you didn't. But I believe you did take something that belongs to me?'

I shake my head and purse my lips. 'Nah you're mistaken I'm not a thief.'

'Well my men here tell me otherwise.'

I look at them both. 'Is that right? What'd I steal?' I shrug my shoulders and turn my question back to the guy behind the desk.

'A woman.'

I laugh, glancing at the two guys beside me, before I turn back.

'You mean the woman they were beating on when I was getting changed?' He looks at them both with a glare before his eyes settle back on me.

'That would be the woman in question, yes.'

I shake my head and shrug my shoulders. 'No clue where she went. I went back into the changing room to wrap my other hand, but it was too late and I had to fight without it. I didn't see where she went, she your daughter?' I don't think she is at all, but I'm trying to bluff my way out of this mess. He doesn't answer, in-fact he doesn't acknowledge the question, he just goes on like I didn't speak at all.

'I am going to ask again and this time I'd like the truth.' He talks to me as though he's talking to a small child.

'I told you, I went right back into the changing room after I knocked these two on their asses. It's not right you know, to treat a woman like that. I don't know where she went. I come here for the money, nothing more. I certainly don't come for the fucking women.' I laugh, because there generally aren't that many decent ones. There are the occasional fuck bunnies, in their fur coats and expensive shoes, clinging to a man's arm three times their age, as they fawn all over them like they're actually in love. Not my kinda girl.

'So you don't know where she went? You have no idea?'

'That's correct sorry.' I shrug.

'Okay. Sebastian, see him out. And, Dominic, if I find out you're lying to me, there will be consequences. Are we clear?'

'Crystal,' I tell him as I walk out of his office.

***

Chloe

My head is so cloudy. They've been forcing pills down my throat for the past week to keep me quiet and asleep. Mainly so I don't attempt to escape again.

I pretended to be asleep when the big oaf came back to give me another dose. The moment he turned to open the door, I bolted. Seeing as my vision isn't very clear and my legs are super wobbly, I didn't get very far. That bastard smacked me across the face, but then the man from the fight the other night showed up and saved me. Thank God!

'Hey, lady! Do me a favour and try to stay conscious back there. We're almost there.' The cabbie's voice jolts me awake and I sit upright, somehow manage to knock my head into the handrail on the way.

'Damn it that hurt!' I mumble to myself.

'Sorry ma'am. I just didn't want to have to call someone to come get you and you looked like you were about to take a little kip in the back of my cab. Anyway, we're pulling in now.' He points up to the two story brick house to our right. 'The gentleman paid me to make sure you got in safely, so go on up and I'll wait out here until you get in the door.'

'Thank you' I reach and open the door, and start to head up to the house. Only to lose my footing because of the bulky clothes and my foggy head, landing on my knee. I'm sure I'll have a huge bruise come the morning. Hands reach under my armpits and start to help me up.

'Here, miss let me help you to the door.' The driver helps me along the pavement.

'Thank you so much for your help. I truly appreciate it.' He knocks and a young woman answers the door.

'Hi. You must be Dom's friend? He told me to expect you. Come on in. I'm Zoe.' For some reason, my heart sinks. I shouldn't be bothered that he has a girlfriend. And she's stunning, which doesn't surprise me because he is absolutely godlike. Dom! Even his name is perfect!

The cabbie leaves and I follow her into the house. 'Thank you for letting me stay here for a bit. I'm Chloe Richards.' She leads me to a sitting room that has a huge television on the wall that's playing the Alibi channel. I sit down on the sofa and that's when I notice an older lady sitting in a recliner asleep.

'Let me just take her into her room, and I'll be right back.' Zoe turns and rouses the lady from her slumber, and helps her down the hall. The aftereffects of the drugs are taking a toll on me. I must've dozed off as soon as she walked away, because next thing I know I'm waking in panic. My head feels better and I can think clearer. I need to get out of here now. These people don't deserve me bringing all this trouble. For all I know, those two goons could have followed me and could be making their way here right now. I have to get out of here before any harm comes to Zoe or the older woman, whom I'm assuming is an elderly relative of one of them.

Even though my clothes stink, are filthy, and have a couple rips, I can't keep on the clothes Dom put me in. Now that my head is clearer, I know just what I need to do. I untie the long belt thing he put around my waist to keep the pants up and take them off. I fold them neatly and then last minute decide to keep the hoodie on so I have something to cover my face if need be. Making my way to the door, I pull the hood up and turn the knob to make my way out. Just as I get through the entryway, I run into a brick wall. Hands reach out and grab me before I fall backwards.

'Where are you heading off to?' I look up into the most beautiful root beer coloured brown eyes and realize it's Dom's arms I've landed in. I'm having a hard time tearing my gaze from his, but I know I need to go.

'I'm sorry I shouldn't have come here.'

'You said you're in trouble, let me help you.'

'But what if they've followed me or even you? I don't want to bring any danger to you, or your girlfriend.' He nudges me back into the house and closes the door behind him.

'Hey, there you are.' Zoe says as she walks towards where we stand in the hallway. 'I went back into the living room but you were out like a light. Then heard talking so thought maybe you were up. Hey, Dom. Glad you're back. Your nan is all set in bed. Surprise, surprise, she fell asleep watching Castle again.' She laughs and makes her way to the coat rack grabbing her jacket and purse from the peg.

'Thanks again for keeping an eye on her. You're a godsend, Zoe!' He hugs her. She opens the door and makes her way out.

'You know it's no problem and I'm happy to help out. It was nice meeting you, Chloe.' she waves disappearing around the corner before I can respond.

'So, Zoe is your nan's carer?' I know I shouldn't be concerned with this right now, but I can't seem to get my mouth on board with my brain.

'She's my neighbour and helps take care of Nan on the weekends when I have a fight. But she doesn't know that I fight, so I'm hoping you didn't say anything to her?' He wrinkles his nose.

'No, no! We barely spoke. When we came in your grandmother was asleep and she took her into her bedroom. I must've fallen asleep on the couch for a bit. When I woke I figured I probably shouldn't be here so I was on my way out the door.' I try to move around him to the door, but his arm comes out and blocks my way.

'Why don't you fill me in on what's going on and if I don't think I can help, you can be on your way.' He walks, into what must be the dining room and sits at the table. I follow, the last thing I want is to sit, so begin to pace back and forth. I don't know what to do. 'I personally think we should be calling the police since you said that you were kidnapped. But honestly, I'm not hot about them finding out I'm an illegal fighter. If you'd like to call, I can take you to the cafe down the street and you can call from there?'

'No! Please don't contact the cops. I just really need a phone so I can get a hold of my father.'

I stop pacing. We can't call the police... I need to contact my dad and see what's going on, let him know he's in danger. Even though we don't talk, I can't lose him. He's all I have left.

'Do you have a phone with international calling I can use?' I ask. 'I'll pay you back for any charges. I just really need to call my dad and he's in the U.S.'

'Yeah, you can use my mobile. And don't worry about the charges, I just want to make sure you're safe.' He pulls his phone out of his pocket and slides it across the table to me.

'Thank you, Dom!' I dial out my father's number and listen to it ring and ring until I get voicemail. 'Uh. Hi Dad. Um, I kind of have a situation over here need to speak with you as soon as possible. You can try me back at this number but I don't know how long I'll be here, and I don't have my cell. I'll try to call you again as soon as I can. Be careful and watch your back. I love you.' I blink rapidly, trying to stop the tears from falling. Once I think I have my emotions under control,

I turn back to Dom and take a seat at the table next to him, handing him back his phone.

'Okay, I guess I'll start from the beginning. I'm Chloe, Chloe Richards, I live on Annandale road in Lewisham. I was taken from right outside my home. I think it's been a while, but honestly I can't be sure, because I don't even know what day it is.' My head feels fuzzy just trying to get all the pieces to slot together. 'They've been pumping me full of drugs, and I haven't been able to keep track of the days. The day I was taken, was the day I saw you take down that other fighter, without even breaking a sweat. Pretty impressive.' I tell him with a small smile, trying to make light of how truly scared I am at the moment.

'Alright. I'm Dominic Colton. Where they kept you is only about four streets away from your home. Today is Friday, and it was last Friday I first saw you getting dragged into the back room at the fight. So, it's been a week.' I see his fists clenching open and closed on the table and his jaw tightens. 'I tried to get to the back room to see what was going on and why they were dragging you away. But they wouldn't let me through. I'm so fucking sorry. I knew something was going on and I should've done more to try to get to you. I should have done more.' He slams his fist into the table and rises from the chair so quickly it falls over and crashes to the wooden floor.

'Dom, it's not your fault. This is on my father.' I suppress the urge to get up and calm him. 'It's the reason why I need to get a hold of him urgently. Not only is he in danger but he's the reason I am. That's why they kidnapped me. They're trying to get back money my father apparently stole.' He finally stops walking holes in the floor, his full attention back to me. 'But they didn't do their homework because my father and I are estranged, and have been for over three years now. I tried to explain that, begged them to let me go, but they weren't listening.'

Dom's phone starts to ring on the table, he glances at it and pushes it over to me. 'I'm assuming that's your father' I quickly grab the phone and hit the little green circle.

'Daddy?'

***

Dom

The relief in Chloe's voice is evident when she hears her dad's voice. But it soon turns to anger. Her voice drops an octave when she says, 'So where does that leave me, Dad?' She goes quiet for moment, while he speaks on the other end. 'Right... uh huh... okay... so again, what am I supposed to do?' She stands and starts pacing. 'They took me from my home, Dad. I can't just go back there and get on with my life, I'm hiding at... a friend's house at the moment...' she looks up at me and gives me an awkward smile. 'Yes I'm safe here for now.' She huffs out a huge exhale. 'I can't just stay here... this is your mess and I'm in the middle of it again!' She makes a growling noise in the back of her throat and I think she's going to lose it. I'm way off though because instead, she hangs up the phone and clutches it between her hands. I take her in, watching her unnoticed, while she stands with her eyes closed, as if calming her very soul from within. Until I find myself staring into hazel coloured orbs that stare right back at me. Busted. Her face is turning black and blue where the bastards smacked her around. But her beauty is still clear, even with the blood and swelling. It's a moment before I avert my eyes. I feel like an asshole. She's just escaped being kidnapped, and fuck knows what else, and here I am gawking at her like a horny teenager. I slide the chair back and cringe as it scrapes against the wooden floor like nails on a chalk board.

'Sorry,' I tell her pathetically.

'For what?' she asks with half a smile. I tilt my head and smile back. She knows full well what I'm apologising for. I've been caught like a deer in headlights, gawking. I'm just about to say as much when a loud bang echoes from upstairs. Shit. I sprint up to nan's room only to find her picking herself up from the hallway floor between the bedroom and the bathroom.

'Nan wait a minute, let me help you.'

'Oh, Dominic I don't even know what happened. I was just coming from the loo and then poof, I'm on the floor.'

'Nan, you're supposed to use the frame so this doesn't happen, remember?'

'Oh, I don't need a walking frame, I'm perfectly fine. It's just a one off, nothing to worry about.' She says like it's not the millionth time she's fallen.

'Have you hurt yourself, it was a pretty big bang you went down with?' I ask, putting her back to bed.

'I'm full of aches and pains, dear, it's old age you know.' I tuck her in bed and leave her with the bedside light on.

'If you need anything else, Nan just let me know. Do you remember how to use the intercom?' I'd had it installed because she often likes to go up to bed early and watch her TV there. A lot of the time she'd come down, but I couldn't risk her trying to do stuff for herself and so got the intercom fitted. It cost me a fortune but it's worth it. The next thing I need installed is a stairlift. I've got all the brochures but they are a small fortune, and I'm yet to find one I can afford without a monthly payment plan. When I'm back down the stairs I find Chloe in the lounge. The TV's off and she's just sitting there looking at the blank screen. Her head turns though as I walk in the room.

'Is she okay?' she asks, as I walk around the sofa and sit

I nod sighing. 'It happens a lot. She forgets she isn't good on her feet.'

'Forgets?'

I nod again. 'She has dementia, she had a stroke about a year ago and since then her left side is weak. It's affected her brain functions, so although she's with it most of the time, she does have trouble remembering stuff. The main thing being that her body doesn't quite do what she *thinks* it's capable of doing.'

'Oh my, I bet it can be exhausting at times.'

I give her a small smile, she's hit the nail on the head. 'It is, and that's why I fight at the weekends because she needs around the clock care and I can't afford to pay someone to be here twenty-four seven, and honestly I prefer to do it myself. Plus, I have this place to pay for, but... that's another *long* story, for another day, you must be tired out?'

'That's very noble of you. Not many men would consider caring for a grandparent like that,' she says, and I think I see sympathy in her eyes.

'It's the least I can do. I practically grew up in this house with my nan and grandad as parents. My grandad worked away at sea until a late age, so a lot of the time it was just me and Nan. She made sure I had everything I ever needed, and just about everything I ever wanted within reason.' I chuckle as I think back to the BMX she bought me, and how over the moon I'd been to get it. To this day I don't know how she afforded it. But that was what she did for me always.

'It's still very noble.'

I smile at her words. 'You make me sound like a Colton in shining armour. They're noble aren't they?' That gets a giggle from her and under the circumstances, I see that as a good thing.

'Well you *were* my Colton in shining armour, remember?'

I laugh this time. 'I hardly think that counts,' I tell her, smirking.

'So, what would equate to a rescue then? I'm pretty sure I was being held against my will and you came to my aid when I needed saving?' Her head tilts to the side and she raises her eyebrows in a *you better admit I'm right kind* of way. I shrug my shoulders not really having much to say on the subject, because she is right and I don't want to tell her that just now.

'You see!' she teases when I don't reply.

I look at her again and find a smug smile on her lips. Her face changes and a small frown replaces it. 'Ouch, this sucker is really starting to hurt now,' she says cupping the bruised side of her jaw. 'Stop making me smile,' she orders, like I have control over her facial muscles. I smile back and stand to go to the medicine cabinet in the bathroom.

'I'll grab you some painkillers,' I offer.

'Oh no, I'd rather not. It's just with everything they gave me I'd rather cleanse my system.'

'Shit, I didn't think about that, sorry.'

'Nothing to be sorry for, just…' she trails off and I'm not sure what she's going to say so I wait, but when nothing comes I ask because curiosity gets the better of me.

'Just what?'

Her eyes close as she takes a deep breath before exhaling on a long sigh. 'I'm kind of stuck with nowhere to go and I really don't know what the hell I'm going to do?'

'Well surely you didn't think I'd be all noble and save you, just to throw you out on the street in your hour of need? Come on!' I mock offence.

'You don't know me and you have enough on your plate without my added trouble.'

'Okay, number one, not your fault you're in trouble, number two, I've told you I'll help and I will.' I hold my fingers in the air as I count them off. 'Number three, we have plenty of time to get to know each other because you won't be leaving the house anytime soon, okay?' Her jaw is slack, but she says nothing. I cock an eyebrow in question waiting for her to argue with me. When she doesn't I stand. 'Good now that's cleared up, I'm going to take a quick shower, because I stink, if you're hungry help yourself. I'd kill for a sandwich if you're making one!' I wink as I leave the room.

***
Chloe

'Make me a sandwich!' How arrogant is he? I can't help but smile as he turns his back and heads up the steps to shower. I can truly admit, I've never met anyone like him before. No man goes out of his way to

involve himself in something like this, that could bring trouble to his front door. And he doesn't even know me. I'm a complete stranger to him, but I can't deny the pull I have towards him and if the way he studied me earlier is any indication, he feels it too.

I head over to the fridge and start rustling around in it until I find some turkey and ham lunch meat, sliced cheese, lettuce, and some hot mustard. As I start to set everything out on the kitchen island, the gravity of the situation hits me. My dad was no help at all. He said he'll take care of everything and not to concern myself with it, and to just stay put.

How can I not concern myself with it when I've been thrown right in the middle with no choice? They kidnapped me... I can't even go home... And now I've imposed on these kind people's lives... I don't know what to do, but I know I can't stay here for too long and continue to put them in danger. I'll just stay the night to gather myself together and then figure out what I can possibly do in the morning. After I call my father back and see what he's pulled out of his ass.

Chloe

'MIND IF I join you?' Dom asks as I'm making my way to the table with two plates in my hands.
'Well I succumbed to your demand and one of the sandwiches is yours, so I hope you do.'

He laughs as I set the plates on the table, turning towards him with mock anger on my face. 'Do you mind grabbing something for us to drink first, sir?' Messing with him may have been the wrong thing to do because he immediately stops laughing, and his mouth forms a straight line. The desire in his eyes is apparent.

He turns on his heels and heads back into the kitchen. 'Wine, beer, or a Coke?' He glances over at me and I can't help but notice how quickly he reigned it back in, going right back to his normal self. So, for now, I'll just leave it be and not poke the bear. I have bigger things going on at the moment. I think I'm still in shock, honestly. I haven't really given myself time to process what's happened to me.

'I'd love a glass of white wine please,' I ask in my friendliest voice and take a seat at the chair where I'd set my sandwich.

'Coming right up.' I bite into my food and a couple minutes later he joins me with two glasses of wine in hand, setting one in front of me, then taking his seat.

'Thank you for being so hospitable. I really appreciate it. Granted, I don't know why you're doing all this for me, but I appreciate it nonetheless.'

'Well you need help, right?' He asks in between bites of his sandwich with an eyebrow raised in question.

'Uh... Um... Well yes, I do, but that doesn't make it your responsibility. I may not know too many people in this country, but I'm sure I can get in contact with one of my friends and go stay...'

'No,' he interrupts me. 'I said I would help you and that's exactly what I'm going to do. Anyway, didn't I hear your father say to stay put when you were on the phone with him?'

'Yeah, but I can't keep putting you and your grandma in danger. That's not cool with me, no matter what my father said. I'll call him back in the morning, and see what he's done to change this horrible situation he's put all of us in.' I look up at him and take a sip of my wine. I'm impressed with the wine. It has the perfect amount of sweetness to it.

'You can use my mobile to call him.' He gets up and starts to clear our dishes and put them in the sink.

'I can wash those. I don't want to make a mess in your home.'

'No, that's not necessary. You made the sandwiches, I'll clean the plates. Why don't you take your glass of wine to the living room and flip the TV on and I'll be in there in a few minutes.'

***

Dom

'If you're sure.' She smiles.

'I'm sure. I won't be long.'

She smiles again as she walks away. She needs a shower and some fresh clothes but she still looks hot as hell. I watch as her ass sways with each step she takes. I'm still watching her walk the length of the hall as she turns and catches me. I'm standing there, like a fucking jerk, with a dirty plate in each hand. As I turn away I catch her biting on her bottom lip. *Jesus Dom, get your fucking act together.* Acting like she's the first woman I've seen in years. Well it's not far off. Since I've had my nan to care for and I moved in here, there has been a total of... maybe four times I've had sex. Not many people want to know you when you say 'sorry I can't stay out too late because I have to get back to my nan.' Yep they go running. So, apart from the handful of times I've taken one to the bathroom in a bar, there hasn't been anyone. Definitely not someone I'd invite back to the house. I wash up the plates and make my way back to her. I find her sitting on the edge of the sofa, like she's uncomfortable.

'Hey, you okay?'

'I'm fine, I think.' She smiles nervously. 'Do you mind if I jump in your shower?'

'No, of course not. I should have asked you earlier, I'm sorry.'

'Thanks.'

'I'll show you the way.' I lead her upstairs and to the bathroom. 'If you want to hand me your clothes I can put them through the wash?'

'Umm yes please, thanks, but… I don't have anything else?'

'Shit no of course, wait a sec and I'll be back with something.' I run to my room and rifle around trying to find some joggers with a pull cord, and come up with nothing, they are all fucking huge for her tiny frame. I open up my t-shirt draw and pull out a whole bunch, all extra large. I take them because I assume on her they'll be like a short dress and cover everything she needs covering. I'm just about to leave my room, when I realise she's probably going to need underwear too. Shit. I open my boxer drawer and look for a particular pair that doesn't fit too well since I bulked up. I know they have to be there somewhere. The very last pair I pull out of the draw. Finally, I head back and hear the shower running through the door. I knock lightly and hear a nervous little yelp. She's no doubt still jumpy. Understandable.

'Yes?'

'It's just me.' The door opens and she's standing there wrapped in a towel, her clothes in one hand the other on the door handle. I take her in. Her neck and collarbone are bruised too, reminding me again what she's been through this last week. I juggle all the clean stuff into one hand and try to take her dirty laundry with the other.

'Thank you, but I can put them in the laundry if you would just tell me where it is?'

'That's okay honestly, I don't mind doing it.'

'I would really rather do it myself.'

I shrug because it's no big deal if she's uncomfortable with me washing her stuff, she can do it herself.

'Okay no worries, but your knickers would be safe with me, I prefer cotton boxers to tight lace, they chafe.' I wink and smile. It makes her giggle and I turn away wondering whether I should have said that given the circumstances. I take one last look at her as she smiles and closes the door. 'I'll be in the living room, just let me know if you need anything else. They aren't much but they're the best I've got.' I tell her as she peeks out of the small crack in the barely open door.

Biting her lip, she smiles. 'Thank you.'

I make my way back down the stairs and wait for her in the living room. I'm tired as fuck after the fight so I pull the lever at the side of the sofa until it reclines to just the right angle. I must doze off, because I wake up to Chloe nudging my arm. I sit up and quickly realise she isn't at all because she's also fast asleep, her head resting on me. The TV must have timed out again, and the room is dark except from the light coming from the hall. I check my phone. Shit it's four a.m. I think about leaving her to sleep on the sofa but quickly change my mind. My nan likes to be up bright and early, so it's best I put her in the spare room upstairs. I debate on carrying her up. The likelihood of her waking while I try to lift her is high, and that would make for an awkward situation. Not wanting her to freak out on me, I gently nudge her shoulder instead. A small whimper leaves her lips followed by a low, 'Nooo.' But her eyes don't open. I try again, and I get nowhere. I figure she must be exhausted and go with my original plan of carrying her up the stairs. I slide my hands under her body and as they get all the way under I tilt so she rolls up my arms, and against my chest. Jesus, she's light as a feather. I stand and move toward the stairs. I get her all the way to the spare room without her making a murmur. I try and rest all her weight on my right arm and knee so I can free up my left to turn the doorknob. Easier said than done, she's light but it's awkward. I finally manage to free my hand and the door opens. I don't flip the light on because I don't want to disturb her, so I pull back the duvet using my knee for balance again, and lay her down. She immediately curls up in a ball as I cover her with the duvet. A small smile creeps onto my face as I watch her. Shaking my head, I realise I'm like a fucking pervert standing over her like this. I leave the room quickly. My room is just next door but I want to make sure all the doors are locked and all the windows secure before I go to bed. Bit fucking late now mind you, but better late than never. I have several weapons stashed around the house too. Not out in the open but hidden with easy access. You can never be too careful. And the game I'm in, you never fucking know who will come after you.

CHAPTER FOUR

Chloe

I WAKE SUDDENLY, with a sense of panic, wrapped up in a strange bed, but my nerves quickly settle when I realise that I'm still at Dom's. I can't find it in myself to move it's so comfortable. For some reason, it gives me a feeling of security knowing he's here. The smell of bacon drifts through the door and my stomach lets out a loud growl telling me to feed it. Stretching I slowly sit myself up and check out my surroundings. The room is small but it's decorated tastefully in simple florals. There's a full bedroom set in a beautiful oak and a TV set on top of the armoire.

Dom must have finished washing my clothes because they are set folded on the dresser. I swing my feet over the edge of the bed and make my way to them. I definitely need to get some more clothes from my place if I'm going to be staying here for a while. And from my talk with Dom last night, I'm not going anywhere just yet. I'm really scared they'll find me, but I'm even more scared of putting Dom and his family in danger. But for the moment, I'm not left with much choice. I'll have to get in touch with my father and hope that he can take care of everything, and quickly with Patrick Smith.

Cautiously making my way down to the kitchen, I turn onto the hall and come face to face with Dom's nan. 'Good morning, ma'am. I'm Chloe. Dom let me stay the night last night.' The scowl on her face tells me that he didn't tell her I was here. 'I'm sorry if I'm intruding. He assured me it was alright.'

'Dommm,' she screeches and I jump back. He comes rushing around the corner, spatula in hand. 'Dom who's this in my house?' She asks him as he stands next to her.

'Nan, I told you I had company last night. I'm making us all breakfast right now.'

'You did?' She stares at him a long moment and then her eyes light up. 'Oh yes sugar, I remember now. You gave me quite a fright, young lady. I'm sorry my memory isn't what it used to be.' She moves towards the dining room and takes a seat at the table leaving Dom and I standing in the entryway.

'I'm sorry about that.' He waves his spatula towards his nan.

'It's ok. I completely understand and I hope I'm not intruding? I can go, just as soon as I give my father a call...'

'No, no it's ok. She just didn't recall that I told her. She's knows I'm a grown man and am able to see women if I want.' A warm blush creeps along his face. 'That came out wrong... that's not what I meant...I don't bring women here all the time. Well not ever. I don't have women here.' I giggle as he stumbles over his words.

'Calm down there, Romeo. I get it. Is something burning?'

'Oh shit.' He turns and bolts back into the kitchen to tend to whatever is stinking up the place. I follow him and can't help but laugh as he smacks the toaster upside down into the sink to dislodge the bread.

'Thank goodness it wasn't the bacon,' I say while laughing. I pick up the spatula off the counter and move to tend to the eggs. 'I'll just finish cooking the eggs while you deal with your burnt toast issue.'

'Burnt toast issue, huh?'

'Ahhh!' A jet of cold-water lands right on the small of my back and rolls down my butt crack. 'Oh my god I can't believe you just did that! It's on, Dom, now it's war!'

His eyes connect with mine 'Challenge accepted.'

***

Dom

I didn't sleep too good last night so I'm tired. I wanted to get up early and make sure I was up and ready before Chloe got up, I don't want her to feel awkward around the house. And honestly, I wanted to make sure she didn't up and disappear. She seems a little different this morning, her attitude maybe? Not so scared. But I'm not an idiot I know it will take a while.

'You sleep okay?' I ask as I serve up our plates. Nan is in the living room so I prepare to take hers in to her. But I wait for an answer first.

Our eyes meet and she smiles. 'I did, I slept like a baby.'

I laugh. That saying confuses the fuck out of me. 'You know that saying is all wrong, babies don't sleep too good they have their parents up all night long.'

She giggles. 'I guess you're right, I've never given it much thought.'

I'm an idiot. Why the fuck did I even say that at all? Now she's going to think I'm a smart-ass.

'But I did sleep really well, thank you surprising really considering… everything.'

'Good. I'll be right back just going to pop a plate in to my nan.' She nods and I leave the room. Finding my nan already starting to nod off in her chair.

'Hey, nan, I've made you some breakfast.' Her head bobs up and she smiles.

'You know, Dominic you don't have to cook for me. I should be cooking for you, you're such a good boy.' I smile and wonder how old the version of me is, she's referring to right now.

'I like to take care of you, Nan you know that.'

'I know. Is your girlfriend joining us for breakfast, Dominic?'

'Um, yeah Chloe is my friend, she's in the kitchen you want to come sit with us?'

'No, no, you don't want an old woman cramping your style. She's very pretty, Dominic.' She smiles.

'She is, Nan.' I smirk because I know what she's doing.

'It's about time you had a woman to look after you.' Always with this, she's relentless, she was like this with Zoe for years.

'It's not like that, Nan, you can come sit with us if you want?'

'I'm just fine here, Castle is about to start.'

I nod and make my way back to the kitchen. Chloe I'm sure heard the whole thing because she is beet red and sniggering into her hand. I roll my eyes and sit in the chair opposite.

'She's relentless.' I smile as I pick up my fork. 'Sorry if you heard all that.'

'You don't need to be sorry she's sweet, and she thinks I'm pretty.' A huge smile erupts and she flutters her eyelashes as she laughs. I'm debating telling her that she is very pretty but the smile drops from her face, and I realise I've been staring at her for the last minute without saying anything. Fuck me.

'She's right.' I tell her and shovel scrambled egg into my mouth. Her face flushes and I smile knowing I've affected her.

'Um, wow. Thanks,' she says, embarrassed.

'Sorry, I don't mean to embarrass you.'

'Dominic, please stop apologising you haven't done anything wrong, quite the opposite, I feel like I owe you a huge apology for dragging you into all this. You've been nothing but kind from the moment you found me. I know I would still be there if it wasn't for you.'

I swallow the eggs and try to smile. Instead I kind of grimace and nod. But she gets the idea. 'So I guess I'm trying to say thank you and sorry all at once.'

'No need to be sorry I told you already you didn't ask for this.'

'I'm so grateful, Dom, I can't even tell you, but I do need to get away from you and your family it's not fair on you.'

I groan. Not this shit again. 'Chloe, we had this conversation last night. I told you, and you agreed, you are going to stay here until shit is sorted.'

'Dominic, I didn't agree, you did. I just feel—'

'Nah, you need to listen to me and stay put, you have nowhere else to go. I'm not letting you go and get hurt. Not on my watch.' Something flashes in her gaze and I'm not a hundred percent on what it was, but I watch her for a second more until I finally see resolve in her eyes. I nod and she nods back, not presenting another argument. I watch her as she picks up a slice of toast and takes a bite. God even that is fucking beautiful. Jesus Christ, I have a problem, a case of asshole with a side of blue balls. What the fuck is wrong with me? I'm acting like she's the first woman I've ever seen. I pick up my own toast and distract myself.

'Do you have a girlfriend, Dominic?' I almost choke on my bite. Can she read my mind? 'I'm so sorry I shouldn't pry, I don't know why… it doesn't matter.'

I clear my throat and swallow. 'No I don't.' I tell her watching for her reaction tilting my head I wait for something. Anything. To see if she's interested. Chloe takes a deep breath and nods to herself, before taking another bite of her toast. And I can tell she feels awkward.

Smiling to myself I ask. 'Why do you want to know?' Her eyes widen a little as she tries to come up with an answer.

'Oh no reason… just thought I'd make sure me being here wouldn't be a problem for anyone.'

'And if I did have a woman?'

'Um.. well… I guess… do you?' I grin I can't help but feel smug.

'No, Chloe I'm single, what about you?'

She starts to shake her head. 'No.'

'You're not single?' I ask a little perturbed.

'No... I mean *yes* I am single, I meant I don't have a partner.'

'Okay well I'm glad we got that all cleared up.' I grin as she bites her lip and smiles. She doesn't look at me, instead she pushes her food around on her plate. We finish the rest of our breakfast in an awkward silence. As I place my knife and fork down onto my plate, Chloe gets up from the table and takes my plate and hers over to the sink. I watch her as she squeezes the washing up liquid into the bowl and begins washing the plates and pans I used. I put the kettle on and ask if she wants a cup of tea.

'Yes please.' I grab the cups from the cupboard and put the tea bags into the teapot. I make it this way because my nan always knows if you don't use a teapot. How she knows is beyond me. But woe betide anyone who puts the teabag in the cup. I step by Chloe to get the milk and when I turn back toward her I get a face full of soap sud bubbles.

Chloe falls about laughing. 'I told you I'd get you back!'

'Cute, real cute,' I tell her laughing. I take my nan her cup through and when I get back Chloe is reaching for the tea-towel. I snag it quick, twist it and flick her on the ass.

'Ouch you... shit.' She whisper-shouts as I dance back on my feet to take another shot.

CHAPTER FIVE

Chloe

IT'S BEEN A week since I started staying with Dom and his nan. Surprisingly nan, which she insists I call her, has taken very well to me. We have the same taste in shows, so it really didn't take much for her to like me. I can shoot the breeze about Castle and Law and Order any day of the week. Zoe stopped by a few days ago and brought me some clothes of hers to use while I'm here. She's such a nice woman, I've asked Dom not to tell her much about my situation though. In my mind, the less others know, the better.

I pull myself from the bed in the guest room I've been calling my own for the last week... It's Friday and I know I'm not going to be able to convince Dom to skip the fight tonight. But I'm going to give it my all. My feet make soft padding noises on the hardwood floor as I make my way down the stairs. I find Dom in the kitchen making himself a protein shake.

'Good morning, sunshine.' He turns, greeting me. In the past week, him and I have become very close. He's barely left my side since I've been here and getting to know him more is making me develop feelings that I shouldn't be in this situation.

'Morning, Dom,' I reply as I prop myself up on the end of the counter. 'Do you think we can talk for a minute?'

'If it's about the fight, Chloe, you know I'm not going to change my mind.' He comes to stand in front of me with his shake in his hand. He takes a big gulp and sets the glass down next to me on the countertop. 'Chloe you know I have to go. If I don't, they are going to suspect something. I've never missed a single fight I've been signed up for and besides that, I need the money.'

'Okay, yes I understand that, but what if they come after you? What if something happens and they don't let you go? What's going to happen to your nan then? Please just skip this one fight, Dom, please?' I plead with him. His hand comes up to caress my cheek and I can't help but lean into it. So many times, in this past week I've wanted him to kiss me, to feel his touch on my skin. And a few times I really thought it was going to happen, only for one of us to realise the situation and back away at the last minute.

'Chloe I really do think it's smarter if I go. And you and Zoe will be here with Nan. I trust you ladies not to let anything happen to her. Anyways they'll probably be more focused on me at the fight rather than coming here to stake out the place. Everything will look just like a normal Friday evening here. Don't worry, Chloe. I promised to keep you safe and I will.' Our eyes lock and once again I feel that intense pull to him, the want to feel his lips on mine. The pad of his thumb rubs back and forth on my cheek and I can't pull myself from his gaze this time.

'Chloe...' My name comes out as a whisper. His lips get closer to mine and my head tilts in.

Knock, knock, knock.

He steps back, breaking the moment. 'That's probably Zoe. She called earlier and offered to take Nan for a walk.' he clears his throat and backs away from the counter. 'I'm just going to go let her in. Be right back.' He leaves the kitchen and my hand goes up to my face. I can still feel the caress of his fingers on my cheek. I hop down off the counter just as he and Zoe enter the kitchen.

'Morning, Zoe. How has your day been so far?'

'It's been great. Ever since Dom showed me how to make those protein shakes, I've drank one each morning and added a little energy powder to it. It really gets me up and moving.' She beams.

'Ah. I'm not a morning person at all, so coffee for me please.' I giggle at her enthusiasm.

'Alright well I'm gonna go gather up Nan and get her ready for her walk.' She makes her way from the kitchen and heads towards the living room where Nan is surely watching TV.

An awkward silence falls over Dom and I as we remain in the kitchen, so I bid my leave.

'I'm going to jump in the shower and get ready for the day.' I laugh as I say it. 'I guess I really don't have much of a day to get ready for. I'll be in my room reading after I shower if you need me for anything.' I start to make my way towards my temporary room. 'And, Dom please reconsider,' I plead with him one more time before I turn back, and make my way to gather my things for a shower.

I must have dozed off while reading Fated Love, the third in a series that I absolutely love. Because next thing I know I'm being woken up by Dom shaking my arm.

'Chloe... Chloe. It's time for me to head out.' I roll over and check the time on the clock on the wall. Six thirty p.m.! I've slept almost the whole day away and didn't get another chance to try and convince him not to go. And now he's heading out the door!

'Dom. No. Are you sure? Did you think about all the things I said earlier?' I quickly sit up in the bed and the blanket falls from my shoulder exposing the loose fitting cami Zoe let me borrow. But right now, I don't even care. Dom is my focus.

'Yes, Chloe. I thought about it all. But the stuff that I said still stands. I have to go. It's the only way I can keep my home off his radar.' I feel his gaze burning through me and it heats me to the core. His eyes drop down to my chest and my heart starts to race. He clears his throat. 'Um I do have to go though, right now. I'm sorry. I have to get there to get warmed up and since I haven't been hitting the gym this week, I have to make sure that I'm stretched.'

'Okay but please promise me that you'll be careful and make sure to look over your shoulder. These are bad men, Dom and they'll pull anything that they think they can get away with.'

'I promise, and I'll check in with Zoe after the fight.' He reaches down and pulls me into his embrace.

***

Dom

All day I've wanted to go upstairs to Chloe, but I held back just like I have all week. It's fucking killing me having her in my house and not touching her. But I want her to feel safe and to trust me, not regret anything. After everything she's been through the last thing she needs is me all up in her face, I don't want to go rushing in and scare her, or make her want to leave. I'm pretty confident she feels the same. But maybe it's the situation that has her feeling that way? Maybe the fact I'm the only guy she sees right now is making my case for me, and if she had choices she wouldn't look twice at me. Fuck, I'm driving myself fucking mad with it.

Walking to the fight with my earphones in was a good call. By the time I arrive, my head is in the game and my legs warmed up. I go straight over to the booking in table. The guy sat there looks pleased to see me and writes my name on the board behind him. When the board is filled with who is fighting who, the bets start. It gets really loud then.

I make my way into the shitty bathroom where I change and wrap my hands. I'm first on tonight and winner stays on. I failed to tell Chloe that part, knowing she'd put up a much bigger fight than she already had. They have fights here every night of the week but weekends are where the big money is. So, I make sure I'm down to fight every Friday. Normally I would pop in and check out my opposition, but this week I haven't had time. Well that's a lie, I have had lots of time but I've spent it with Chloe and Nan. I have no idea what I am walking into in the cage tonight. I'm an idiot. But I just didn't get around to thinking about it until this morning.

My hands wrapped and shorts on, I start on my stretches. The door opens with a bang and another fighter, Paul, walks in. I've fought him before and he got a good punch in, but I beat him in the first few minutes. He's never let me forget about that lucky punch though. He's a nob head but I humour him.

'You know who you're fighting tonight?'

I shrug my shoulders. 'I'm on first, that's all I know. Winner stays on, though.'

'Fuck really? How'd you know? I didn't know that was tonight.'

'Yeah last Friday of every month.'

'Shit, I'm going to see if I can get in at the end.'

'Fucking, wimp,' I yell as he heads to the door.

'Fuck that I'm not going on early if it's a winner takes all, I want paying.'

'It's a big money night you get five ton a fight win or lose.'

'But what do you get if you win the night?' He stops at the door.

'Five thousand.'

'Seriously?' he asks and I nod. He leaves the room, no doubt going to get his name as far down the list as he can. Prick. I didn't get a choice and I didn't argue it.

A bang on the door signals my time is up and I need to head to the cage. I make my way down to it and scan the crowd as I always do. Tonight though, I'm looking for any sign of trouble from the guys I saw last week. Nothing so far. I do what I usually do and don't speak to anyone.

Getting into the cage I realise my opponent is a new face. He looks mean as hell, and ripped too. But that doesn't mean he can fight. I sidestep around the cage, dancing past him. He looks nervous but focused on what he has to do. I don't take my eyes off him as I pass him a second time. He puts in his mouth guard and turns his back to me. I decide to shake my arms out up close and personal, trying to psyche him out. He doesn't turn but I know what it feels like and he will know I'm there, breathing down his fucking neck.

It's all part of the game. And if you can't take it, you shouldn't be in it. It's that simple.

The referee does his usual speech between us, holding one of our hands each. We touch fists and the fight is on.

The ref sticks to the edges of the cage, well out of our way. The guy in front of me starts to do all sorts of stupid shit—spinning and jumping around, trying to hit me, expelling all his energy and hasn't hit his mark once. I love fighting guys like this. I'm a street brawler, I'm not professionally trained in any way. But it's how I make my money so I make sure I take anyone down. This idiot is jumping around like a fucking monkey. And I'm pretty sure he just hissed at me. I watch him for a few more seconds and the crowd starts to get annoyed that no hits have been landed yet. I watch for his tell. He kicks to my head and it's at that precise moment that I strike, he's wide open when he swings his leg up and out. I pull my arm back and I punch him using all my body weight behind it.

Crunch.

His nose pops and blood goes everywhere. He wobbles on his unsteady legs, I move in with another punch... He goes out like a light. The ref runs to him waving his arms letting the crowd know he's done. I stay where I am, watching as four men drag him down the cage stairs to wherever they'll dump him. I kneel at the far end of the ring waiting to see who comes through the gate next. I'm not given much of a rest before my next opponent arrives. I've fought him before, he's a good fighter and one I will have to be on my A-game for this one. Within a few seconds I'm fighting again. Standing in-front of me is five hundred quid that I need to pay the bills. I have to win. I just need to keep my wits about me and fight sensible. He comes at me first and I dodge his efforts. He's swinging hard and fast and trying for that knockout punch, but I won't be giving him an easy ride. I dodge another and get one in to his kidney as he swings and misses. Then I throw another to the side of his face, he takes a knee but is up again in a few seconds. I stand back allowing him to get up, using this to catch my breath. I could grapple with him and take him out, but that kind of fighting saps your energy fast, and I don't want to burn myself out. So I wait. His fists come up in a boxer's stance, so I use my legs, a body shot takes the air out of him. His arms come down to protect his ribs leaving his head open so I move in. Three jabs and an uppercut takes him down. He didn't lay one blow on me. The crowd erupts and I kneel again as he's carried out. The third and fourth fight are pretty similar to the first two—except I'm much more tired and losing my focus by the fourth. I take some hits and end up with a swollen eye. Sweat dripping into my eyes stings like a motherfucker. But I've had worse. I have no choice but to grapple and by the time number four goes night, night, the crowd are screaming like fucking animals and I'm fucked. Fight number five is my final fight thank fuck. Paul comes in looking all fresh as a daisy. Fucker. I groan a little as he starts to do punch combinations in front of me. He's a dirty fighter and I'll need to make sure I don't let him get one on me. He's smaller than me but not by much. I get to my feet and go toe to toe as the ref talks to us both. He bumps my fist and we're good to go. I've already made two and a half grand so if I do lose, it will be okay. But… I don't like to lose. My ego doesn't take it well.

 He comes at me quickly and I side step. I need this one over with before I'm too tired. I don't take my eyes off him for a second. I follow him round the ring watching him playing to the crowd and showboating like the prick he is. But it's okay he thinks I'm too tired to beat him, so he wanted the easy win at the end of the night. He drops his guard swinging his fist around in a circle showing off and trying to goad me. I laugh on the inside, but I don't show it I stagger around a little making him think I'm worse than I am. As he steps to the side and looks to the crowd for more cheers I attack. He isn't expecting it, and I see panic as my fist hits his face. Idiot. You never take your eyes off your opponent. Rookie mistake. He stumbles because it wasn't a knockout blow. But I make sure my next one is. I hit him with a combination of three. Right left right. He goes down hard and is sprawled out like a starfish.

 That's when the fatigue hits my muscles. I feel like they're locking up on me as the ref lifts my arm and the crowd goes wild. I spit out my mouth guard and inhale trying to get enough oxygen around my body and make my damn legs work better. They cooperate enough to get me to the bathroom and I drink my sports drink and hydrate myself. Then I grab my shake and shake it up gulping that down, I feel full and a bit sick. I look in the mirror at my face and curse, my eye isn't cut but it looks nasty all red and purple and inflamed. I wouldn't be surprised if it closes up. I only remember him hitting me once, but this looks like I got my ass whipped. I get changed and head for the table. There are women in the cage now. Going through the same shit I just did to get paid. I want to get home so I don't stick around and watch. I head straight to the booking table for my money.

'Boss wants to see you,' he tells me.

'Fuck's sake, just pay me my money. I need to get going.'

'I said, boss wants to see you, he'll pay out not me.' I follow him to, *boss man's* office. Four men surround me as I walk through the door. And the smug bastard sits behind his desk. steepling his fingers.

'Dom, you had a good night,' he starts. I don't answer just nod. 'You cleared the ring and earned me a lot of money, I thank you for that.'

'No problem, listen… can I get paid? I have somewhere to be.'

'Such an attitude, Dom. If we're going to work together you need to change that.'

'Good thing we're not then, because you get what you see and if you don't like it fuck you.' I shrug nonchalantly.

He laughs and shakes his head making a noise like a tsk by sucking air in through his teeth. It's gross. 'That's the thing though, Dom, see you lied to me last week, you told me that you didn't take the girl and I know that you did—'

'I didn't snatch no girl.'

'DON'T FUCKING LIE TO ME,' he bellows and spit sprays across his desk. Disgusting. I inhale and sigh.

'How could I kidnap a woman from under your nose?'

'I'm done playing games, Dominic. I know where you live and who lives with you. I know everything I need to know about you. I can ruin your life in the blink of an eye and wouldn't break a fucking sweat, so here is what's going to happen. I am owed a very large debt, and you are going to fight for me every night until it's paid and you will win or lose dependant on what I tell you to do.'

'I won't throw a fight.'

'You don't have a choice, do as I say or the girl dies along with everyone else in your life, Dom. Could you live with that? That's the only question you have to answer. Could. You. Live. With yourself?' He grins and waves his hand at me, meaning I have to leave. As I step back though he starts again. 'I am leaving her with you, only because she hasn't left your house.' I look up realising he has actually been watching us. Smiling he says, 'I will leave her there until I feel the need to bring her back, so in a way you are holding on to my property, let's think of it as a loan, like a hired purchase. You get to keep her as long as you pay but the minute that money stops coming in, she's mine.' I grind my teeth together and when he says nothing else I take another step toward the door.

'Remember, Dom, she can't leave your care. If she does you will pay the price… your grandmother seems like a very nice lady.'

Fucking cunt.

I grind my teeth together but don't say a word. As I open the door, he says 'Your five grand will be a down payment, only one million, nine hundred and ninety five thousand to go.'

'What? I'll be fucking ninety before I can pay that off you said you earned money from bets tonight you have to include that too,' I barter.

He pulls a face, 'For you Dom I will, but only because I like you.'

CHAPTER six

Chloe

I FEEL THE dip as Dom climbs in and wraps his arms around me, pulling me close, and placing gentle kisses on the back of my neck. His hand gently caresses down my abdomen and my legs involuntarily clench closed, as moisture gathers at my core. I crane my neck back and catch his lips with mine. In one quick unexpected movement, he has me under him, grasping my hair in his hand to hold my head in place as his tongue seeks access to mine. His fingers find my sweet spot, he teases around my folds right before inserting one finger in and I moan into his mouth. At this point, there is no way for me to hide just how attracted to him I really am. This man, my saviour. I can't hold back anymore; my hand reaches for his boxer briefs and I push them as far as I can get them. He lifts and kicks them off the rest of the way. My hand seeks out his cock and when I find it I gasp in shock at how big he is. His lips smile against mine as he continues kissing me. He removes his finger and takes his time teasing my entrance with his dick. It hurts at first, but then I give myself to him fully. I sigh his name as he gently slides in and out until he has fully seated himself in me. I moan out his name just as he says mine…

'Chloe… Chloe? Is everything okay in there? Chloe?' All my senses come into focus as I wake to Dom knocking on the door and calling my name with worry in his voice. I hop up off the bed and crack the door open just a bit, hoping that he can't tell I was just dreaming about him and I really hope he didn't hear me.

'I'm up. I'm sorry, I must have been in a deep sleep,' is all I can think to say. I know my cheeks are probably flushed but there's really nothing I can do about that.

'I was walking by and heard you call out my name?' He eyes me questioningly.

'Umm yeah I don't...' I shrug. 'Maybe just having a crazy dream. You know how dreams are, I don't recall what it was.' My cheeks burn redder, knowing I'm telling a bold-faced lie. The wetness in between my legs can attest to that.

'Well okay. If you need anything, I'll be down in the living room with Nan... I may head to the gym later if you want to tag along and get out of the house?'

'Wait, I thought I wasn't able to leave the house?'

'I think it'll be alright. They didn't say anything at all to me the other night. We'll just take extra precautions if you do want to?' He throws out the words to quickly, as if there is more to it, but before I can question it, he's gone. The last few days seem to have dragged. Dom has been withdrawn and I just know there's something going on, but he refuses to tell me. After the fight, my heart dropped when he walked in the house and I saw his eye swollen shut. He assured me it was from the fight and not the goons who'd held me hostage. Zoe and I had spent the next hour cleaning and icing his eye. I swear when Nan saw him the next morning she almost fainted. The care, love, and bond between those two is definitely unbreakable.

My father finally called back yesterday, after a week of me calling and leaving multiple messages. Nothing new. He just kept apologising for putting me in this situation, saying he's working on it and telling me to stay put. I argued with him, telling him it isn't fair to Dom and his family if I stay and continue to put them in danger, not to mention my developing feelings for Dom. But then he asked to speak to him so I handed the phone to Dom and watched as the two men currently in my life talked about me like I wasn't even there. At the conclusion of their conversation, Dom just hung up. Nothing else. My father didn't even want to speak to me again. Dom pretty much just grunted out that I'm to stay put and then left the room with his phone.

And that's where we're at now.

Three days later and no closer to finding a solution or any closer to me being able to return home. I won't lie though, I've become very fond of Nan over the last weeks and Zoe is starting to become a good friend too. My attraction towards Dom just gets stronger every day. The last couple of nights I've dreamt of him. The first dream he'd just climbed in my bed and held me. I surprisingly slept better that night than I have since my drug induced coma the first night at Dom's. And now I'm dreaming of him making passionate love to me... The chills that I still have running down my spine, tell me that I really need to re-evaluate this whole arrangement. But in order to do that, I need to know what's really going on. A workout today is starting to sound better and better.

***

Dom

I get my nan all set up in the lounge and prepare myself a shake. As I leave the kitchen Zoe knocks on the door. Opening up I welcome her in.

'To what do we owe the pleasure?' I ask. Chloe and her seem to have become fast friends.

'Thought I'd come over and pester Chloe and your nan for a while unless you have plans?'

'I'm just going to go to the gym. I'm not sure if Chloe wants to come with me yet, was going to ask you to sit nan if she does.'

'Okay well I guess I'll watch Alibi with Nan if she is.' At that Chloe walks down the stairs with a tiny pair of shorts and a vest top on. My jaw almost hits the floor as she reaches up to put her hair in a ponytail. Zoe elbows me in the ribs and smirks as I come back to my senses.

'Hey, Zoe, you okay?' Chloe asks as she gets to us at the door.

'Yeah thought I'd come hang out for a while, but I hear you're going down to the gym?'

'Yeah, I thought I would, it'll get me out of the house.'

'Well come on then, Zoe is staying with Nan so we can take our time,' I say.

'Oh yeah take it real sloooow, you don't want to rush it.' Zoe sniggers, giving me a sly wink. I can't help but grin because she's a goofball. Chloe looks between the two of us and raises her eyebrows giving us a wide eyed confused look. I smile and open the door.

'Oh shoot I need water!' She says behind me, dashing off to the kitchen. I wait at the front door and look down the street both ways and then again. I notice two guys a couple of drives down and take a mental note of their licence plate. I know we're being watched so it should be easy enough to spot. For a few minutes there, I almost forgot all the shit we've got going on. I still haven't spoken to Chloe about what Patrick the asshole said. Chloe comes out holding up one of my drinks bottles.

'Hope you don't mind me using this?' She smiles.

I shake my head. 'Nah, its cool.'

'You're sure this is sensible? Safe for me to be going out?'

'I'm sure I checked the area while you were inside, not a soul in sight,' I lie, feeling fucking guilty.

We walk in step, but as we near the bottom of the street I feel her looking at me.

'What's up?' I ask.

Shaking her head, she smiles. 'Nothing.'

I frown and prod her playfully. 'It's something and definitely not nothing.'

'I was just thinking this is nice, walking down the street together and being normal you know?'

'I guess.' I smile and she prods me back getting me just below the ribs.

'Oh you wanna play that game huh?' I grab for her and she squeals and picks up her pace. I easily catch her though and I wonder if she is actually wanting me to capture her. As I reach my arms around her and lift her off the ground she wriggles in my arms and her ass comes into contact with my dick. I quickly drop her back to her feet and she wriggles some more. Practically grinding her ass into my groin. I groan accidentally letting it slip past my lips. And she stops immediately it's like time stood still for a split second. But then I tickle her and she giggles, wriggling free from my grip.

'No fair, you're not allowed to tickle me.' The smile on her face reaches her eyes and I see nothing but pure beauty shining in them. And what's best about it? She doesn't even know how beautiful she is.

'Fuck, you're beautiful.' Her eyes widen and I realise I said that out loud. We turn the corner and I catch her looking at me biting her lip.

'Thank you,' she says smiling. I smile back putting my hands in my pockets because I don't trust myself not to take her in my arms and kiss the fuck out of her gorgeous plump lips. Tension thrums through me.

'It's the truth,' I tell her nonchalantly.

'I'm glad you think so.' It's a nervous smile she gives me.

'Why?' I ask maybe a little cockily.

'Well… umm… because it's nice to be thought of in that way.'

'No-one ever tell you that before?' I find it hard to believe she wouldn't be told that on the regular.

'Not anyone that mattered.' she mumbles.

'So that means I matter?' I chuckle nudging her shoulder with my arm.

'You do, yes.' She looks at me seriously and the humour drops from my face just as quick. Her body is screaming out to me, and all I want to do is taste her lips. We're in the middle of a busy street, people are milling around doing their daily thing but in the middle of all that all I can see is Chloe. Her tongue pokes out to wet her bottom lip and I can't take anymore. I have to taste them. I take her hand and pull her to the side of the pavement, pressing her up against the wall of the greengrocers. Before she can stop me my lips meet hers. I didn't need to worry whether or not she'd open for me because it's instant, like she's read my mind. Her lips part, allowing me entry, and I don't waste a fucking second. As our tongues dance, she moans and her fingers roam up the front of my chest and then around my neck, finally finding their place in my hair. As for my hands, they go straight to her ass and I'm not even one little bit ashamed of it. It feels amazing finally having her in my arms. As the kiss comes to an end, I let her go and we stand smiling at one another, like two teenage kids who got their first kiss.

'So... umm where's the gym?' she asks a little breathless.

'Oh yeah, its ahh...' I try and gather my thoughts. 'Just up there and we take a right.' I take her hand and pull her from the wall. I make a point not to drop her hand and she doesn't let go, so I see that as a victory. I thread my fingers through hers and look to her for any kind of awkwardness, finding nothing. We get to the gym and I sign Chloe in on a day pass.

'You know what you're doing on the machines or do you want some guidance?' James one of the personal trainers asks her.

'I got her.' I tell him.

Clearing his throat he steps back. 'No problem, just doing my job.' He smiles at Chloe. 'If you need anything just let me know.' He winks, like I'm not standing right here.

'Fuckwit,' I grumble under my breath.

'What?' Chloe asks.

'Nothing, let's go to cardio and warm up.' She follows me and I set up her treadmill and then step on the one to her right.

'You want to speed up or slow down just use those buttons there, these ones are the incline.'

'Okay I'm ready to rock.' She giggles. I set mine up and it's not long before we are working up a sweat. Normally I zone out in here and listen to music but today my mind is everywhere but in the zone. I feel like I should confess to Chloe what's going on. I have two more weeks till the mortgage needs paying and not to mention all the other bills, and I have no income coming in now, and have to fight every night. But then I look across to her and a huge smile splits across her face. I don't want to spoil that, today. And tonight isn't a fight night because it's Sunday. I want to pull her off that fucking treadmill and work her out in more ways than one. I need to calm myself down.

'I'm going to go and throw some weights around you staying or you want to come?'

'I'm not going to lie,' she says. 'I'm nervous as hell being out of the house, but I guess it's quite safe here?'

'It's very safe, no-one can get in unless they're members and I won't be far just there.' I point. 'I can see you, I promise.'

'Okay, well I'll run for five more and then I'll come over to you.' I watch James like a fucking hawk when I leave her there. Thankfully he doesn't go over. But I see him watching her. I grind my teeth together and start on the leg weights.

CHAPTER SEVEN

Chloe

I POP MY ear buds in, putting the music on low so I can still hear my surroundings, and I watch Dom going hard on the free weights. Even with Jack Beats *Knock You Down* in my ears and running at a steady pace on the treadmill, I can't seem to peel my eyes away from his reflection in the mirror. And that kiss... Oh my. I've definitely never been kissed like that before. It was like no one else in the world existed. He could have taken me right there and I wouldn't have had a second thought about it. My dream did not do him justice. My mind should be more focused on my surroundings right now, making sure I'm safe, but I can't help watching his muscles ripple as he pulls the weights up and down. And I really believe that I'm safe with Dom here.

My eyes meet his and I watch Dom's eyes go wide as someone taps me on the shoulder. I jump out of my skin and almost fall from the treadmill terrified. I glance over to see James the personal trainer standing next to the machine. I regain my balance and curse under my breath, pushing the button on the treadmill to slow my pace. My heart races for a few seconds, a combination of fear and a reaction to the alarm on Dom's face. I breathe a huge sigh of relief and take my ear buds out.

'Hi, Chloe right? Sorry I didn't mean to scare you.'

'Yep that's me.' I ignore his apology. 'Did I forget to fill something out on the sign in?' I question as I see Dom putting his weights back and heading this way. I saw the way Dom looked at

James when we arrived and he thinks I didn't hear his mumbling on our way to the machines. I know he doesn't have much like for this guy. Does Dom maybe think he works for Patrick or something?

'No, no. Everything was fine. I just wanted to stop by and see if you'd like me to spot you on some of the weight machines over in the enhancement area? Maybe show you the proper way to use the equipment?'

'The only thing you're going to be showing her is your back as you walk the fuck away.' I hear Dom growl from behind me. His arm comes around me as he turns the treadmill off. I hop off and entwine my hand through his, realising he's just jealous and not worried about the guy in a dangerous sense. He glances down at me and I can feel the calm wash over him with just that simple gesture.

'Let's just get out of here, big guy?' I bat my eyelashes at him as a way of encouragement.

'Okay, yeah let's go. There's this little hole in the wall deli a couple streets over that has the best pastrami around.' And with that, we make our way out. I spot James the trainer in my peripheral and he looks none too happy. But hey what can you do? For all intents and purposes, Dom and I are together and I'm alright with that.

The gravel crunches under our feet as we take a back alley to the deli shop Dom's suggested. Our hands haven't come apart and every few feet he stops to kiss me, as if he just can't get enough. I don't blame him because that's all I want right now too. I feel like a high school girl with a crush that's finally come to bloom.

We stop at a random black door with the smallest sign that says Marty's Deli on it and he pulls me through the door. Any other time I would feel apprehensive to go into a place like this, but I know Dom will keep me safe, he already does.

'What looks good?' he asks me over his paper menu, after we've grabbed a corner booth. He thinks I didn't notice him scout out a spot to sit where he can see all exits, but I did.

'You said the pastrami is delicious, right?'

'Best in the U.K.,' he states simply.

'Alright, pastrami on brown seeded for me, please.' Dom goes up to the counter and puts our order in. I can't help but peek at his ass as he walks away. It's like he was sculpted perfectly just for me. Round, plump, I'd like to bite into it. I duck my head real quick as he turns and catches me checking out his ass. When I chance a peek back his way, there's a panty melting smile plastered on his face. Thank God I'm sitting because my legs feel like they turned to pure jelly.

'So what's the plan?' I ask as he takes his seat and divides our food between us.

'You meaning for today or for this whole situation?'

'Well I did just mean for today but now that you mention it, I would like to know if there is any game plan for all this craziness? I'm so tired of putting you and Nan in danger. It's not fair to you at all. I need to leave you guys alone and go back to my regular life.' I gaze out the window and his hand comes to rest on mine, the sensation of his thumb rubbing back and forth fills me with warmth.

'You want to leave?'

My eyes jump back over to him and I can see a mixture of hurt and concern on his face. 'No no, I didn't mean it like that.' I bring both of his hands into mine. 'Dom, I'm really attracted to you. Over these past weeks, I've come to love being with you, Nan, and even Zoe has become a closer friend than I ever expected.' My eyes fall to the sandwich in front of me, willing it to give me strength. 'But the truth is, I've been thrust upon you. I'm stuck in your house, beyond my control, for reasons neither of us created. I was kidnapped by men who could have killed me and probably still can.' I raise my eyes back to his. 'You've been my saviour and still are. But, imposing in your home and bringing danger to your door, that's where it crosses the line. I would have loved to meet you outside of this ordeal so this thing between us could blossom instead of either of us having our doubts because of what we've been thrown into.' He pulls his hands from mine and rubs one hand down his face.

'You have doubts?'

'No, not really, but I was worried you might? It would just really help if we knew what our next move is? What's going to happen next? My dad has been no help whatsoever and this is his damn mess!'

'Chloe, let me just say this. I don't have doubts. At all. And everything is going to be okay. We *will* work through this and we *will* do it, together. I promise I will do everything in my power to not let anyone hurt you or Nan. You guys are safe with me. Just give it a little more time and trust me.'

'I do trust you, Dom, and I will stay. But please promise to be honest with me about what's going on if anything happens at that place.'

'Will do.' He takes a bite of his sandwich which ends our conversation on the topic. 'I've been meaning to ask, where's your mum at in all of this?' He throws out with his mouth still half full.

'She's been gone awhile. It's just been dad and I for quite some time, but that's a story for another day.' My excitement about my delicious looking pastrami sandwich evaporates as I look down at it. My appetite has gone. So I just get up and start gathering the garbage to toss.

He grabs my hand and we head out the door towards home. It's only a few streets away and when we get up to the door he stops and turns towards me.

'Chloe, I care about you, and fuck, am I attracted to you. I just want to be real clear that it's not this situation that's brought that about for me. The first night that I saw you, when I was in the ring, I felt it. That's what pushed me to follow and see what was going on. I know this isn't the ideal time, but when this is all over I'm going to take you on a date, that okay?' I don't respond. Instead I pull his tall frame down to mine and plant my lips on his. Could he be the first one I give everything to? I pull his bottom lip into my mouth and nip gently until I feel his tongue poke out to soothe it.

We break apart at the sound of someone clearing their throat only to look up into the doorway and find Zoe stood there with a big ole smile plastered on her face.

'Alright you two lovebirds, break it up. Nan wanted to know when you'd be getting back. She's starting to get antsy and is going through all her old recipes. And you know how crazy the kitchen will get if we let her cook.'

***
Dom

Trying to get my nan down from her crazy high is a task in itself. I'm trying to wrestle the whisk and bowl from her as she flicks through her recipe cards with her free hand.

'Nan, we don't have the ingredients to bake today, I need to go to the store.'

'Oh, well then will you get me what I need for an almond cake please?'

'Sure, sure. I'm going a little later on, but right now I need a shower, why don't you go up to bed and have a nap?' It's a long shot but when she's in this state of mind it's the best thing for it, because nine times out of ten she wakes up a lot better. Chloe is standing in the doorway a little unsure of what action to take. I smile as I finally get the whisk free from Nan's hand.

'I am a little tired.' She smiles at me.

'Okay Nan, let's get you to bed.' I roll my eyes at Chloe as we pass and she smiles.

'I'll be in the shower as soon as I've put Nan to bed. If you need one too I don't mind sharing.' I shoot her a wink. 'I'd hate for the hot water to run out,' I whisper. Her eyes widen and she bites down on her bottom lip. I'm not sure if I'm pushing my luck, but fuck it, I've been skirting around it for long enough now. And I'm hoping she joins me.

I get Nan into her room and it takes about ten minutes until I get her settled with her telly on and tucked up in bed. As I make my way to the bathroom, I grin as I see Chloe leaning up against the wall by the door. I stop and tilt my head as her tongue peeks out and wets her lips. And that's it I'm done. I move in covering her mouth with my own. She tastes so fucking good; her hands roam up my chest and around my back pulling me in closer. I reach around and pull her ass in so her body is flush with mine. My hard on undeniable between us. Her breath hitches as I end the kiss.

Opening the door, I pull her in. Lifting her onto the sink vanity, I capture her mouth again. Her hands slide up my arms and then down my stomach where she grabs the hem of my t-shirt and pulls it up, I shift away and lift my arms for her. Her eyes widen as she takes in my chest and each tattoo. I give her a few seconds before I try and get her equally undressed. Her arms raise as I lift her top, giving me access to her more than ample breasts. I stop and stare at her small lacy black bra, and my mind goes to thoughts of a matching set. I don't wait, or even ask permission as I latch my lips around her nipple through the thin material. Her moan only spurs me on further and I push both cups down under each breast giving me unfettered access. I pinch one nipple between thumb and forefinger while I swirl my tongue around the other. Her head goes back against the mirror and her eyes close as she mewls from my touch. I pull back and put my fingers into the band of her shorts. Waiting, asking for permission. It's granted as she lifts her ass off the counter and allows me to pull them over and down. Leaving only a thin slip of material covering her pussy. I groan as my dick tenses at the thought of what's to come.

I step back and take her in completely. So fucking beautiful. Her eyes open and she looks at me with a gaze full of need. I drop to my knees and her hand covers the place I want to be. Frowning I try to move her fingers.

I hear her giggle. 'I need a shower before this goes any further, Dom.'

'The fuck you do let me in.' I try again, her giggles fill the small room.

'Hell no, Dom I've been to the gym, let me clean up first.' I groan and roll my eyes, making her giggle again. I get to my feet and strip her thong from her body and move to her bra, flicking the hooks open.

'Wow you've done that before, huh?' I don't answer her. Nothing good could come from that conversation. Instead I take her mouth again and lift her into my arms. I pull my shorts and boxers down with one hand while holding her weight with the other. I kick them off before stepping into the shower and I turn the tap on. Cold water cascades over us.

'Fuuuck.' I grit out through clenched teeth. While Chloe laughs her ass off. It warms up pretty quick but I barely notice because I'm captivated with her lips. I let her go to her feet, sliding her down my body, my erection standing proud between us. I reach behind her grabbing the shower gel. Squirting just enough into my palm I rub my hands together and start at her shoulders. Getting the sponge, I move it over her skin in slow circular motions and as her eyes close, her head rocks back against the wall. She mewls again setting my body on fire. Her fingers roam down my chest and to my vee, almost grasping my dick, but I stop her. I want to make sure I'm cleaned up first too. I sponge her down and as she frowns and starts to protest about not being able to touch my dick, I drop the sponge and use my fingers along with shower gel on her pussy. Chloe stops her protest as quickly as it began as my fingers toy with her entrance. I take some more gel and get to my knees, as my nose hits her bare pussy I take my dick in my hand and rub the gel in. As I lap at her pussy she moans in relief. Her eyes closed, her head tilted to the ceiling.

'Look at me,' I demand as I insert a finger. She does and as I pump faster and flick her clit with my tongue her eyes don't leave mine. She starts to pant and it isn't long before her walls start to clench around my finger. I flick faster and harder and as she goes over, I replace my finger with my tongue and lap up her arousal. It's then I realise I haven't got any condoms in the house. I stand resting my forehead against hers and wait as her breathing comes back to normal.

'Fuck me you're hot,' I tell her honestly.

'That, what you just did... that was hot.'

'Chloe, I can't tell you how much I need inside of you right now, but I don't have any protection, sorry.' I'm so fucking mad at myself.

'Me too but...' I watch her get to her knees her hands slowly moving down my body until she grasps my cock in her hand. 'We don't have to stop,' she whispers then takes my dick and swirls her tongue around the head. Fuuuuuuuuuuuuk that's good.

Dom

CHLOE AND I had an amazing night together. Despite not being able to have sex we managed more than once to get each other off. But more than that we talked a lot, about our parents, our childhoods, school friends and more. I feel like we've really hit it off.

It was a perfect opportunity for me to come clean and tell her what had happened at the fight ring. But she seems so happy and comfortable at the moment. The fear she felt when she arrived has long gone. I don't want that to return. But in order for me to pay off her father's debt and get her free and clear I need to go and fight six nights a week. I can't hide that from her. It often takes my body a week to heal from one fight, so who knows what the fuck I'll be like by the end of the week. What I do need to do is contact Chloe's father again. I spoke to him briefly without Chloe's knowledge and arranged to call him again today at nine a.m. which I believe is four in the morning for him. I look over to Chloe still sleeping next to me in my bed. I've never had anyone in this bed before and I'm surprised, but it doesn't feel wrong. I smile thinking back to last night. I was so close to just taking that risk and fucking the life out of her. But it wouldn't have been right. Especially since she isn't on any kind of contraception either. That stupidly makes me happy, because that means she didn't have reason to be.

I watch her for another minute until the bathroom door closing distracts me. Nan is up. I don't want her going down the stairs without me to help, so I kiss Chloe on the forehead and put on my shorts heading down the corridor to the bathroom.

'Hey, Nan, you okay?' I ask knocking lightly on the door so I don't frighten her.

'Of course I'm alright why wouldn't I be?'

I smile to myself, she forgets she has an en-suite. 'No reason, Nan just checking you're okay.'

I get to the kitchen and make Nan her morning cup of tea. And while I scoop the coffee into mine and Chloe's mugs she walks through the door, looking sleep mussed and beautiful.

'Hey.' She smiles sheepishly.

'Hey, yourself.' I walk over to her tilt her chin and kiss her lips. As I pull back she bites her lip, and I feel my dick stiffen in response.

'How'd you sleep?'

'You have a very comfortable bed.' She smiles.

'Snoring didn't bother you?'

'Snoring?' She frowns.

'Yeah you snore really loud, I don't know how you sleep through it.'

'I do not.' She giggles and smacks my arm. I grab for her and tickle her making her giggle louder, as she wriggles free I hear nan clear her throat behind me. As I pull Chloe flush to my chest Nan smiles and asks if I have mashed the tea in the pot.

'Yeah, Nan as if I'd make it any other way?'

'Well it tastes like crap made in the cup.'

'You worry far too much, Nan. I've been making you tea since I can remember, I learnt from the best didn't I?' Smiling she walks back into the living room. I feel Chloe relax against me and realise just how tense she felt during that conversation.

'You okay?' I ask.

'Yeah, I just didn't know what to do with myself when she walked in.'

'What do you mean?' I smile.

'Well we were messing around and she might think...' She shrugs.

'That you slept in my bed and gave her grandson the best blow job? I doubt—'

'Dom!' She squeals with wide eyes and flushed cheeks. I laugh loud at her embarrassment. Looking up at the clock, I realise I've only got about thirty minutes until I call Chloe's father. I need an excuse to go out. I pour the tea and add milk to the coffee before taking the kettle and filling the mugs. I hand Chloe hers and she mmm's in pleasure as the smell hits her nose.

'You needed that huh?'

'Ugh like you wouldn't believe. I'm not a morning person.'

'Really? I'd never have known it.' I smile sarcastically, she is like a bear with a sore head until after her second coffee, something I have picked up over the last couple weeks. However today she seems in a much better mood. Maybe it was the multiple orgasms? Whatever it was, she has a smile on her face and a blush to her cheeks. And I like it a lot.

'Okay so this morning I have some errands to run, pharmacy and a few things to collect from the store anything you need?' I ask.

'Maybe some…' she stops to look around. When she's happy Nan isn't listening she whispers, 'Some protection?' She bites that fucking lip again.

'Oh believe me that is top of the list and why I'm going to the store.' Still biting her lip, she nods shyly. I sip my coffee and place the mug down next to her. With my free hands, I take her mug and slide my fingers to the side of her neck caressing that sweet spot behind her ear. Releasing her lip with my forefinger, I close my lips over hers and savour the coffee taste that swirls around with our tongues. Her hands trace the muscles in my arms until she gets to my biceps and then she squeezes them and I know it turns her on. It's not the first time she's done it, even before we crossed that bridge. It was there whenever she looked at me, her eyes would drink them in like a fine wine on a palate. I'm suddenly aware of the time, it's flown by. I swear it feels like only five minutes have passed but it's been almost thirty. As I step back she grabs for her mug, taking a huge gulp.

'If you like, I can go with you?'

'That would be great but I have no one to watch Nan, would you mind?'

'Oh of course, I'm sorry I should know by now.'

'Hey.' I tilt her face up and look deep into her eyes. 'You know I don't expect you to care for her, it's just easier than going for Zoe right now.'

'Oh I don't mind at all, it's the least I can do to help, and not because I feel I have no choice. I love being around her, please don't ever think that I wouldn't want too.'

'I don't.' I smile. 'She really likes your company too.'

'Really?'

I nod and smile at her surprise. 'Really, believe me if Nan doesn't like someone she doesn't hide it.'

'I can imagine.' She giggles. I kiss her quickly on the lips, just a small kiss, that turns into three more small kisses.

'I'll be back just as soon as I'm done.' I wave going into Nan and kiss her forehead before leaving through the front door. I wasn't joking when I said I was headed to the pharmacy. I need to buy condoms and not a small box. I check the time, three minutes until I'm supposed to call. Fuck it. I call up his number and hit send, putting the phone to my ear, I wait as it rings on the other end.

'Yes,' a short voice snaps.

'It's Dom.'

'Who's fucking idea was it to call me at this time?'

'Yours,' I tell him honestly.

'Hmm, well let's get to business. That fucking gypsy scum has my girl in his sights and he's not willing let her be, yes?'

'Yes. He's saying I have to pay off your debt and then he'll leave her alone. But I don't trust the motherfucker. It will take me the rest of my life fighting six nights a week to pay. It can't be done, not to mention the fucking money I already had to pay, and I have a mortgage and bills to keep my nan in her own home. If I don't meet that payment in a few days, I'll be in shit street there too.' There is silence on the end of the line for a few seconds.

'How much do you need?'

'I'm down five grand.'

'And what is that in dollars?'

'I don't know, it's five thousand pounds?'

'I'll wire it to you today, so that problem's solved. I am unable to leave the country at the minute but I can send you some men.'

'I don't need men I need your debt paid.' I raise my voice a little and realise I'm in public when I get side glances from a passer-by.

'Listen to me, I do not owe that cocksucker a fucking dime. He made a bad call and now he is looking for a patsy to take the fall, and that patsy it seems is me or you.'

'Why would he lie?'

'No the question is, why would I? You have my only daughter, she has been kidnapped once and is still under threat, so why would I lie to you?' I think on that for a minute.

'Do you have the money to pay him off or not?'

'No—'

'For fucks sake.'

'But I do have contacts and men on hand, we can deal with the situation in a manner that would suit and benefit us both.'

'You mean kill him?'

Silence. 'Listen fighting is the only way I can look after my nan and keep a roof over our head, so killing him wouldn't benefit me.'

'The time for fighting for your own gain is over. I know this man better than you can imagine. He has you where he wants you and you will never be able to win or lose a fight again without his say so, and you will never see a nickel or dime of any winnings. No matter if I paid him in full.'

'So he needs to be put down.'

'Yes, like the fucking scum pig that he is.'

'You two have a lot of history?'

'Oh yes we do, and the fact that he has the balls to take my daughter proves he is still as stupid as he was all those years ago.'

I take a deep breath, fuck me, what have I got us into. 'Okay so it's decided. What do you need me to do?'

***

Chloe

Dom has been off training for the last few nights. I've been asleep when he's returned and in my own bed because I didn't want to be presumptuous and wait in his bed. I'm kind of bummed out after the night we spent together. It was beyond my wildest dreams, even though we didn't actually have sex. When I woke the next day, I felt like I was on cloud nine. Now it seems as if he's distanced himself from me. He's not backed off completely, he still kisses me and shows affection. But each morning I've woken to him having new bruises or cuts. When I ask him what's going on, he just says it's from his training and that he's been sparing. And then he's withdrawn from the conversation one way or another. I truly believe something is going on, but I don't know how to get him to open up to me. And him giving me the cold shoulder when I bring it up isn't helping.

'Hey, Nan, what's on the telly tonight?' I ask her as I bring in a bowl of popcorn and some nuts, setting them on the coffee table. Tonight, is the fourth night in a row that it's been just us, while Dom has been off at the gym training. I love her company and I love watching the Alibi channel with her but there's only so much Castle one person can take. The other night I tried to put on The Gifted and she just about ripped me a new asshole.

'They have a Law & Order: SVU marathon going on so I figured I'd get my fill of pervs and sickos being taken down tonight,' she says.

The cashew I just tossed in my mouth gets caught in my windpipe and I start coughing to dislodge it. Nan waddles over laughing and gives me a smack on my back.

'Nannnn. Who taught you to talk like that?' I ask once I'm able to breathe again and catch my breath.

'Oh honey, I've been around since before your parent's parents. I've seen it all and heard it all. Besides, what I said just now wasn't even remotely bad. The type of stuff they film on that show happens in everyday life. There are so many horrible people out there in this world. That's why I took Dom under my wing when he was young. His parents didn't know what was best for him and I didn't want him to grow up to be like his asshole father. I wanted him to be a well-rounded and respectable man.' She tosses some popcorn in her mouth and has a sad look on her face as she chews. I don't even know what I should say to that. 'It pains me that he sticks around here to take care of me. I know he should be out there living his life and meeting beautiful women like you. But I've held him captive for so long now and I truly don't know how to survive without him.'

I cringe at her word choice. *Captive.* Just as I was held captive and Dom was the one who swooped in to rescue me.

'Nan, I don't think it's anything like that. Dom loves you dearly and I can see his love for you every time you're together. I don't think he'd leave even if he could. You did the best for him and now he's going to do the best he can for you.' I set the bowl of nuts back down on the table and angle myself towards her. She has a pained look on her face and her hand is cradling her arm. 'Nan, are you ok?' She doesn't respond and I grab the house phone to call Dom. Just as I get back to her, the phone ringing in my hand, she drops to the floor and her whole body turns a blue. I hang up the phone and dial 999.

'Nan, Nan. Please, Nan just hold on.'

'What's your emergency?'

'I think my friend is having a heart attack or a stroke or something. Please, please send an ambulance quickly.' I practically scream into the phone while cradling Nan's head in my lap.

'Is she still breathing?'

'Send someone out here now.' I'm panicking so I try to take a deep breath. 'Yes, she's still breathing. Please send someone out here right now.'

'Please calm down, miss. I'm dispatching an ambulance right now. Stay on the line while you wait for them to arrive.' The other line beeps through and I know it has to be Dom.

'I have to go. Her son is calling.'

'Miss don't han...' I click over to the other line as quickly as possible while still trying to rouse Nan and not jolt her head around.

'Dom, Dominic is it you?' The words quickly fall from my lips.

'Yes. Chloe. What's wrong? Why are you panicking?' I cut him off as he tries to continue.

'Dom it's Nan. Something is wrong with her. I called for an ambulance.' I hear a big crash and the line goes dead just as the EMT's arrive and start banging on the front door.

'Come in,' I scream almost at the top of my lungs. Two men come rushing in. I get asked a bunch if questions as they push me out of the way and check Nan's vitals. It all goes so fast and the next thing I know, I'm following them into the back of the ambulance. I throw out a silent prayer, Dom please get here quick and please God let this wonderful woman be ok.

CHAPTER NINE

Dom

I'D LITERALLY JUST got my hands wrapped and was getting in the right headspace to fight. I always turn my phone on silent but tonight I needed some music to get my head straight.

A missed call was flashing on the screen…

I run all the way home and find Zoe out front with a look on her face that I don't want to interpret.

'Where is she?'

'They've taken her to The General, Dom, it didn't look good. I wanted to go, but wasn't allowed in the ambulance as well. Chloe is with her though.' I pull my phone out and call for a taxi, pacing up and down getting more and more desperate with every passing moment. When the guy pulls up, I almost rip the door off and climb in. I bark out which hospital and turn to find Zoe has climbed in the back seat. She tells him calmly to go as fast as possible. We seem to hit every red light and my frustration grows.

'Just put your fucking foot down.' I tell him as he slows for an amber light. 'I'll pay double what the meter says if you get me there quick.' His foot goes down and we just beat the red light. And that's how the rest of the journey goes.

As we pull up, I throw a twenty at him. I don't even close the door. I don't wait for Zoe. I sprint to the reception desk. I give Nan's name to the woman who looks like she isn't in any kind of hurry to check anything. She doesn't even look at me, instead she continues her conversation with the clerk sitting behind her. I wait a beat of a second trying to calm down. But when the woman starts to tell her about the guy who she went on a date with, I lose my shit.

'Sir, if you don't calm down, you will be asked to leave.'

'How about you do your fucking job!' Security comes over and I roll my eyes.

'Look can you please just tell me where my Nan is at?'

'Well, why didn't you just say so?'

'I did.' I answer through gritted teeth. Zoe's hand grips my arm, I glance in her direction and she mouths 'calm down,' with a slight shake of her head. I inhale through my mouth and exhale through my nose, calming myself, as the woman taps the keys on the keyboard, searching for my nan's location.

'Bay twenty-four in the ICU.'

'Where is that, please?' Zoe asks.

'Take a left through the double doors, left again and then at the second set of doors there's a buzzer. Wait until answered and they will direct you from there.' The woman immediately goes back to her previous conversation with the clerk behind her.

As we wait to be buzzed through the door, all my anxieties about losing Nan seem to crash into me. I falter in my step. Zoe notices and grabs my arm telling me everything will be just fine. Zoe has lived next door for so long, I don't remember anyone living there before her. The look on her face tells me she cares a fuck load about my nan, and somehow that makes me pull my shit together. I have to be strong for my nan.

My phone starts to buzz, but I ignore it. Everyone I care about is here already. The nurse in charge leads us to my nan's room. Looking through the window my heart drops, Chloe is clutching Nan's hand in her own, and the tears are streaming down her face. My nan looks grey. Like all the colour has been sapped from her face. I can't move my feet for a second. My eyes meet Chloe's as' I walk through the door.

'Oh, thank God, Dom.' Chloe exhales in relief. 'They haven't told me anything yet. They just did a bunch of tests and said they need to take her for a scan soon.'

'I'll go and find a nurse.' I tell them both.

'No, Dom you should stay with her, I'll go and find someone,' Chloe says.

I nod and as she walks towards me, she sobs again. 'She just went down Dom.'

'Hey, hey it's okay, she's gonna be fine.' I wrap my arms around her and kiss the top of her head. As she pulls back and looks at me, I give her a chaste kiss on the lips. 'Thank you, for getting her here.' I take her seat as Chloe leaves to find a nurse while Zoe takes the space to Nan's other side. We don't speak, we just sit listening to the sounds of the machine beeping.

'She's going to be okay, Dom,' Zoe tells me with a sad smile. I nod because in that moment looking over my nan laid in the bed looking even more frail than usual all I can think about is what I'd do without her. And how selfish that is. My phone starts to vibrate continuously, so I take it out and answer it aggressively. 'What?'

'You ducked out on our agreement, Dominic, that doesn't bode well for you and your little family, where the fuck are you?'

'Listen, I had an emergency, I'll be there tomorrow.'

He laughs menacingly through the phone. 'You have one priority, Dom. I made that clear, you broke your word, now you pay the consequences.' I look over at Zoe, but decide to say it anyway.

'Listen I'll be there tomorrow, I'll throw the fight, I'll do whatever you need me to do,' I plead with the motherfucker like a bitch, when all I want to do is put his greasy ass face through the nearest wall. Zoe looks at me like I have two heads, as she realises I haven't been truthful with her.

'Oh I know you will, Dom, I own you now.' He hangs up the phone before I get a chance to react. I grip the phone so hard in my hand that the case cracks. Chloe walks in with a nurse and I stand offering my hand. Chloe comes over and takes hold of my other hand.

'Mrs Colton is very lucky to be with us right now,' the nurse starts. 'It was touch and go while the EMT's were dealing with her initially.' My legs wobble like jelly and I stumble back into the chair. 'They believe she's had a heart attack. And the ECG's show that it wasn't a small one.' I scrub my face with my hands. I can't fucking believe this. 'But she is stable right now and they're trying to make sure it doesn't happen again.' Chloe rubs my shoulders trying to reassure me, as the nurse clears her throat. 'The doctor will be along soon to speak to you in more detail, and he also wants to talk to you about a DNR.'

I'm in shock I think, so I just nod my head and agree, not realising the seriousness of it until I look at the girls and find their faces dropped in shock. As the nurse leaves us, I turn to them both.

'What's a DNR?' My mind isn't firing on all cylinders right now, and my brain can't make a connection to the words the nurse said. I turn to Chloe who looks like she's going to burst into tears again, so standing I look to Zoe instead. She looks at her feet as she answers.

'It means do not resuscitate, Dom.'

'Jesus Fucking Christ.' I grip the end of Nan's bed as my feet no longer feel like they can bear my weight. It's that bad. I might still lose her.

***

Chloe

It's been two days since Nan had her heart attack and we've been at the hospital nonstop. Zoe and I went home to shower and bring some things up here, but Dom hasn't left her side the entire time. The look on his face when the seriousness of her condition hit him, broke my heart to pieces. I wrapped my arms around him, trying to comfort him as much as possible.

The doctor came in this morning and gave us her test results. A sigh of relief passed through all of us as he told us that it wasn't as bad as they first assumed. Just a daily regimen of new medicines to go along with her current meds and a new diet. He said that they're going to start reducing her sedatives so she will begin to wake and then they will see how that goes. They want to keep her here for at least another week to monitor her and see if any of her current daily meds interact negatively with the new ones. Which I definitely think is smart, because you never know how a person may respond to combining medicines.

'Dom, I think you should go home to shower, charge your phone, and maybe get a little bit of sleep,' Zoe says as she stands behind him and rubs his shoulders. 'It's been a long couple of days.'

'But what if she wakes? I don't want to leave her.' His hands reach out to entwine with his nans.

'Zoe and I aren't going anywhere, Dom. You'll be our first call if she wakes and we'll be by her side the entire time. I promise.' I can't help but to try to put him at ease.

'You know what, Chloe? I'll be fine here by myself, why don't you go with him?'

'You sure, Zoe? I don't mind staying with you.'

'Yeah totally sure. When you guys get back, I'll head home for some R and R myself and catch some Zees.' She practically pulls Dom out of his chair and takes his place. 'You two get some rest.' Zoe gives Dom's ass a whack as I manage to guide him from the room.

My hand finds his and I can feel his hesitance. 'She'll be ok honey, we'll make it quick.'

The taxi ride back to the house is quiet and tension crackles in the air. I have no clue what to say to console him, so I just say nothing at all. We pull up to the house and he practically throws the money at the driver and hops out. I thank him and follow Dom in.

'I'm going to put my phone on charge and jump in the shower.' He grunts like this is the last place he wants to be and I don't blame him.

'I'll put you a sandwich together for when you're done.' I start to head to the kitchen but his hand on my arm stops me.

'Don't worry about it, Chloe, I'm not very hungry.'

'Okay.' And with that he heads up the steps, the bathroom door closing a moment later. I want to go to him, be there for him, but what if it's time alone that he needs? I push that thought aside and fix myself a glass of iced tea. Moments pass, oh forget this, I'm going to him.

I undress and slip into the shower behind him as he washes his body. Taking the shower sponge from him, I continue where he left off. I can't help but admire how the suds trail down his back as the water rinses them away. His body is truly remarkable. There's so much that has happened to this caring genuine man and I can't help but feel guilty for some of it. My head comes to rest on his back, my arms wrapping around him. Sensing him sag into my embrace, makes me feel a little better that he finds comfort in my presence.

Dom turns and I have to unclasp my hands for him to make it all the way around to face me. There's sadness in his gaze but also unmistakable need. Before my mind can even wrap around that thought, his lips are on mine, his tongue begging to be let in.

My arms instinctively go around his neck and pull him closer. Our tongues rage war in one another's mouths. In one quick swoop, he pulls me up and my legs wrap around his waist. Shower forgotten, he carries me across the hall to my room and gently lays my naked, dripping wet body on the bed and just looks down at me. The hunger in his eyes sends tingles down my spine and caused wetness to pool between my legs. I spread my legs open so he can see just what he's doing to me and he lets out the sexiest growl I've ever heard. Hands trailing up my thighs, his lips and tongue follow. I lose all control over my body and my hips buck as he gets closer to my pussy. And thank God he doesn't keep me waiting. His tongue caresses my folds as he goes from bottom to top slowly. I needed him badly, I weave my hands through his hair and pull him right where I want him. I'm pretty sure I hear him let out a soft laugh, but I'm way too turned on to even care. One last caress up my folds and he sucks my clit into his mouth, flicking his tongue back and forth at a quick pace.

Moaning out his name, I can't help but just let go. I feel like I've wanted this, wanted him, for so long that it's just been pent up inside me. As the trembling in my body calms, he reaches over into the night stand and pulls a condom out of the drawer. Sheathing himself with it, he climbs up my body, taking my mouth in one of the most breathtaking kisses. Running the head of his cock back and forth to wet himself, he slowly starts to push inside me, but he unexpectedly comes across a barrier.

'Chloe?' He stills, his brow quirked in question.

'I'm a virgin,' I whisper, barely audible.

'Shit are you sure you want to do this?' His face has morphed into mask of concern.

'I'm sure, Dominic yes!'

CHAPTER TEN

Dom

I HOLD MY weight up on my elbows and just look into her eyes, they're telling me she's sure, and so is her body. I've only ever done this once before and I felt it with my fingers, but I was a school boy then. This time around, I had no clue. The thought of her not having any contraception pleased me, but this little bit of info has me fucking elated. No one, not one single man has been inside her like this. Fuck if that doesn't turn me on more.

'Chloe, it will hurt.'

'Dom I don't care, I just want to be with you.' I take a deep breath and pull back a little giving myself some room and I slide in slow and firm. As I break through, I take her mouth and swallow a little gasp from her, I move so damn slowly it almost kills me, but I want this to be as painless as possible. I find myself seated all the way inside her, quicker and easier than I expected, resting my head on her shoulder I groan.

'Jesus, you're tight.' I pull back and slide back in taking it easy, her hands find my ass and she grabs it pulling me in that little bit harder. I laugh as she lifts herself up to meet my thrust too.

'Any pain?' I ask her not letting her take charge, biting her lip she shakes her head.

'Good, now let me take care of you.' I lick up the column of her neck as I thrust again picking up my pace. Her hands find my hair and she grips it hard. I thought she was tight to start with but now, as her walls contract around me, it'll be a miracle if I don't come in seconds.

Jesus she feels good. I pull out and she looks like she wants to smack me in the face. I pull her quickly so she's on top of me. With her straddling me, I line myself up and pull her down onto my dick. Like a natural, she starts to move. And my balls tighten as my head hits the headboard. Fuck she's good at this. A few more strokes and I feel that tingling. Fuck, I lift her up and off me.

'I'm sorry baby, but you are just a little too good at that and I need to take my time with you.' I lay her back below me—her eyes full of need. Lifting her knee to her chest, I push inside and the moan I get in response is so damn hot. I push in harder now and pick up my pace. This time I'm going to blow. But I know she's come twice already, so I need to get her ready to go with me. I push my hand up in between us feeling for her clit, putting pressure on it is all it takes.

'Oh… Oh… Oh, my God.' She pants in my ear as I take her with me over edge.

I kiss her lips as we both come down from our release. I hold my weight above her not wanting to pull out but knowing I have too. There is a little blood on the sheet from switching positions and as I pull out she notices it. Her eyes widen and she starts to apologise. I hold her face between my fingers and thumb and kiss her lips.

'Don't worry about it.' I kiss her again.

'But—'

'Chloe.' I look her in the eyes and smile as she stops protesting and bites her lip. 'It only happens the first time and I intend to do that again and again and again.'

'Oh really?' She giggles.

'Oh definitely.' I lift her from the bed and take her back to the shower which is still running and steaming up the bathroom. I take the sponge and wash her gently between her legs which she giggles at.

'Dom, I can do that.' She tries to take the sponge from me.

'But I want to.' I keep a firm hold of it and bring the sponge up and around both breasts, making my point. 'I'm going to take care of you and you're going to let me.' I capture her mouth to end any protesting.

***

We get back to the hospital refreshed and much happier than when we left. I've yet to turn my phone back on. Zoe would have called the house phone if she needed me. I just want to bury all the other shit for the time being. I know that when I do turn it on, the shit will hit the fan. I guess I'm burying my head in the sand. As we arrive at the room

I find a police officer outside. My heart races and Chloe stiffens beside me.

I run down the corridor and look for my nan who is still in bed in the same state she was when I left, then I see Zoe being tended to by a nurse. Her face swollen and cut. The officer at the door stops me, putting his hands on my shoulders not letting me enter the room.

'Sir, calm down you need to step aside.'

'That's my nan in there. What happened?' I struggle with him to get in the room and Chloe's hands wrap around my wrist.

'Dom, stop please, it's not helping.' I stop struggling and look at her as she takes charge of the situation.

'Officer, that's our family in there and we only left a couple of hours ago, what happened?'

'Miss, I can't tell you anything just yet, I need to question the lady first.'

'But surely you can tell us something?'

'My colleague is with the nurse who walked in, we will know more then.' He nods toward the other officer inside the room.

'Walked in on what?' I shout, but no one is listening. 'Fucking tell me what happened?'

'Sir, I need you to go take a seat in the family room. When I'm done questioning I will come find you.'

'Not a fucking chance before I know what happened to Zoe and if my nan is alright.'

'There has been an assault but I can't elaborate at this time. If you don't calm down and go where I've asked you to go, I won't be able to get any more information for you.'

'Thank you, officer,' I hear Chloe say as she moves me away. She pulls me by the hand and I go reluctantly.

'What do you think happened?' she asks me, looking terrified.

'Looks like she's been socked in the face.'

'You don't think..?' I know what she's thinking and I'm pretty fucking sure that's all it could be. I must look worried because she comes to me putting her hands on my chest. 'Dom, what aren't you telling me?'

I look away knowing this is my fucking fault. I should have kept my phone on.

'Fuuuuuuck.' I growl out. 'They were in her room, Chloe, it was them. Of fucking course it was them.' I punch the wall in frustration.

'I'm so sorry, Dom. I never wanted this to happen, I never wanted any of this for you.'

I turn to look at her. 'Hey… this isn't on you, it's my fault.'

Confusion spreads across her face. 'How?'

'Chloe, I didn't tell you everything, I didn't want to worry you anymore.'

With a deep sigh rubbing my hand down my face I tell her the whole story. When I'm done she sits down shocked.

'So all this time they've known where I was and have been using you.' Her voice is monotone and tears stream down her face.

'But why come here. I don't understand why they've come here?'

'I didn't fight, Chloe. I was there when I got the call and I've been here since. The deal I made was to fight every night. And I've not had my phone on, I just buried my fucking head in the sand. This is their lesson, I play the game their way or I take the consequences.'

'Dom, I need to leave. What if they come back? What if they hurt you next time?'

'Stop it, Chloe, you can't leave.' I shake my head. 'It's not an option, Chloe, not anymore, not now. We'll get through it I swear I'll fix it.'

'Dominic, you shouldn't have to fix this, it isn't your mess.'

'And it's not yours either, but we're in it together and I'm fucked if I'm letting you go, Chloe.' I press my forehead against hers. 'You aren't going anywhere, okay?' She nods against my head and my eyes close in relief. I feel like a weight has been lifted now everything is out in the open, but I hate that she's on fucking edge again. The door opens and Zoe walks in, with a police officer behind her. Chloe rushes to her and throws her arms around her.

'What happened?'

Zoe's face is grim. 'You should sit down, Dom.'

***
Chloe

'Just tell me what happened, Zo. My patience is wearing fucking thin.' The look of worry on his face is enough to break the strongest man. We know he's not angry with her, but it seems as if he could break any moment.

'Alright, Dom.' She takes a seat across from where he's standing, the stress of the day taking its toll on her. 'Nan had just woken up. I was talking to her while waiting for the nurse to get to the room after I pushed the call button.' She inhales sharply, her hand coming up to gently touch the fast-developing bruise on her eye. 'Nan seemed perfectly fine, just like her normal self. Then two beastly looking men came into the room.' She shudders a breath.

'I thought they had the wrong room so I stood and made my way to the door to point them in the right direction, when one of the fuckers hit me, I never saw it coming.' Her face screws up in anger. 'I was out like a light, Dom. When I came to, they were both hovering over Nan's bed and one was holding a pillow over her face. I screamed out at him and pulled myself up off the floor. Just as I charged towards them, the nurse came in, they pushed past her and ran out the door.' Tears are now streaming down Zoe's face, Dom is pacing back and forth, clenching and unclenching his fists. I taste the salty flavour of my own tears as I gasp. My lungs just can't pull in enough air. 'I thought she was dead Dom. Her body looked so lifeless. The doctors rushed in and immediately started working on her…' Before she can finish, Dom charges down the hall towards the elevator. The sound of his shoes pounding on the floor echoes through the hospital halls.

'Dom,' Zoe calls after his retreating back.

'Just let him go, Zoe. I think he needs a breather.' I tell her as I wrap my arms around her.

'I've never been so terrified in my entire life, Chloe. I thought she was dead, Chloe, *dead*!' Crying sobs start to wrack her body as she breaks down in my arms. It takes me a bit to get her calmed down and back to a good frame of mind. When the crying has stopped, we make our way down to Nan's room. There's still an officer outside the door but all the doctors have gone.

'Is it alright if we go in now?' I ask the officer. He nods his head and Zoe and I push through the door slowly, hesitant on what's waiting for us on the other side.

The room is cold and it feels like the first day we were here with Nan. Machines beeping and the sterile smell. We stay awhile just sitting with Nan in silence but I know I need to go check on Dom. Make sure he's alright.

'Zoe, I really don't want to leave you here alone again, but I really need to go check on Dom. I don't think the officer is going anywhere anytime soon. Do you mind staying?' Her eyes go wide but as she glances out the door, the officers arm is visible, and she relaxes a little.

'Go ahead, just as long as he doesn't leave.' She points to the officer at the door.

'Okay, I'll go speak with him and be right back.' I make my way to the doorway to talk with the policeman. He reassures me that there will be someone posted outside the door for the entirety of Nan's stay, until the culprits are found. Which in this situation, could take a while. I relay the same to Zoe, pulling her into my arms for another hug, and then making my way out of the hospital, hopping into the first cab I see to head towards the house.

I've been sitting outside Dom's door for the last thirty minutes with Zoe's phone in my hand repeatedly calling him with no answer. When the taxi pulled up, I could tell that he wasn't home. The lights were still off from when we left after our intimate afternoon together. I went in just to make sure and checked all the rooms. After giving up on my search of the house, I came outside, hoping he'd just show up. Now I'm just sitting here staring down the dark street, the only lights are from the outdated street lamps that have seen better days, as they flicker occasionally.

I'm lost in thought and worry when my phone starts to vibrate in my hand. I glance down assuming it's Zoe again, calling for another update, but am surprised when it's Dom's name that flashes across the screen. I'm all thumbs, fumbling with the phone, trying to hit the little green talk button.

'Dom. Dom, I've been trying to call you. Where are you?'

'I'm fine, Chloe, you can stop calling.'

'Dominic, please just come home.'

'They tried to kill my nan, Chloe,'

'Dom... Where are you?'

'I'll be back.' I hear the unmistakable sound of a crowd as he must open the door and I know exactly where he is.

'Dom, please let's talk about this first, don't do anything stupid, just come home Dom? Dom? Please?' It's useless though because he's already hung up.

Dom

AS I WALK through the doors the crowd is baying for blood. The fighter in the cage looks to be on his last legs, his face covered in blood. But I'm not interested, I have one aim and that's the fucker who calls himself Mr Smith.

I scan the crowd once and then again for good measure. I don't see him, so I make my way to the office in the back. There isn't anyone at the door like usual. So I go right on in. It's empty the place is messy as fuck, papers piled high in the corner, shit strewn across the desk. But it's just the same as the last time I was here. I check for any signs of where he might be. Rifling through his paperwork on the desk. All I find is an abundance of betting slips and random notes that mean nothing. I was certain I'd find him here, and the fact I haven't has me all twisted up. All this pent-up anger and frustration needs an out. I had all my hopes pinned on finding him here and now I don't know what to do. I leave the office and search the crowd once more. Nothing.

I make my way back out to the street and walk aimlessly. Not really paying any attention to where I am or where I'm going, I find myself at home. I open up and shout for Chloe, assuming she'd be there because she'd asked me to come home when she called. Realising she isn't I flop down on the bed. I can still smell us on the sheets. I close my eyes and let the image of her fill my brain. Her lips as she moaned out, her eyes looking directly into mine as she came. Fuck. I sit up fast adjusting myself in my shorts. I can't sit around while Nan is in the hospital. My phone rings, a private number. I almost ignore it but at the last second, I answer.

'Hello?'

'Is this, Dominic?'

'Speaking. Who is this?'

'My name is Andre, I believe we have a mutual American friend'

'Ah okay.' I realise quickly that this is Chloe's Dad's guy'

'We need to discuss business, but I do not conduct business over the telephone'

'No problem, we can arrange a meet up face to face.' I walk out of the house and lock up as I make my way back to the hospital.

'When would be suitable?'

'First thing? Around nine?'

'No problem, I will see you at your house'

'You have the address?'

'I do.' he answers like that was a stupid question. And I have to wonder what the fuck type of guy this is. And do I want him knowing my address? Well I guess it's too late for that now. I'll speak to him in the morning.

All the way I think about what I'd have done if they'd succeeded in killing my nan. The pain in my chest is unbearable at just the thought. I can't deal with it. As I pass through the revolving doors and make my way to the stairs I get an uneasy feeling in the pit of my stomach. I have to stop and take a minute, waiting for it to pass. But it doesn't. Nausea rolls in my gut, but I crack on and make my way to Nan's room. I expect to be greeted by Chloe and Zoe, but only Zoe is there. Nan is awake though and a huge smile crosses her face. I can't help but smile back.

'Hey, Nan, how're you feeling?'

'Fit as a fiddle, don't know what all the fuss is about. Where's your dad?' I frown because usually if she remembers me she knows my dad isn't around.

'That husband of mine is always in the damn pub, you know.' she turns and explains to Zoe. I quickly realise she thinks I'm her son. My dad. Great.

'Well thank you for coming, Son.' She smiles patting my hand and I look over to Zoe who gives me a sympathetic smile. I just sit in silence for a few moments holding her hand.

'Did Chloe not find you?' Zoe asks suddenly, sounding worried.

'No? I assumed she was here.'

'She left to go find you, wanted to check you were okay?'

'I went home because when we talked on the phone I thought she was there. When she wasn't I figured she must be here?' I stand running my fingers through my hair. Shit. I realise she has Zoe's phone, and dial it immediately. I get no answer. I call again and again and it just goes to voicemail each time. 'Jesus, Zo where could she be?'

'I don't know, Dom? Is there something you want to tell me?'

I shake my head no. 'This is so fucked up.'

'Dom what is fucked up? What's going on? You said you'd throw a fight?'

I shake my head again. Not getting into this now. 'I'll go and find her, Zo, but please stay with my nan, I'll be back as soon as I can okay?' I catch her nodding her head as I turn back to my nan. 'Hey, Nan, I'll be back as soon as I can okay?'

'You tell your father to get his arse here, you shouldn't have to sit with me. He'll be propping up the bar no doubt.'

'Okay, Nan I'll do that.' I smile. It kills me inside when she loses time but I know it gets us nowhere to tell her the facts, so I just wait it out and it passes eventually. Hopefully when I return she'll be back to normal. Zoe looks at me, concern written all over her face. I know she has a million and one questions on the tip of her tongue, but I leave the room glancing back over my shoulder as she shakes her head at me. As I arrive in the entrance of the hospital my phone rings again. Zoe's name flashes up. Thank God.

'Chloe, where are you?' I answer.

A sneer I recognise echoes from the phone and I almost lose the contents of my stomach.

'Where is she? What the fuck have you done?'

'Um, call it insurance, Dom.'

'You, motherfucker.' I growl low down the phone.

'Well I sent you a message and you still didn't get it through your thick head. So now you have no choice'

'Let. Her. Go.' I growl through gritted teeth.

'Dom, Dom, I'm a patient man, but you are pissing me off, I expect you here in an hour.' The phone goes dead and my head spins. What the fuck am I going to do?

I head straight to the arena. It takes me a little over forty-five minutes to walk. But I've had time to clear my head. I know what needs to happen. Mr Smith needs to die.

***
Chloe

'Get your grimy, nasty ass hands off me, you you… fucktard.' I yell in frustration as the short, Hulk Hogan wannabe ties my wrists together behind me. 'Steroids much,' I taunt him as I kick my feet out at his attempts to grab them and secure them to the chair. He grunts as my right heel makes contact with his ugly face, he gets up and before I know it, I'm face down on the ground from a smack I didn't expect.

'Kyle, you know better than to touch the insurance policies. Lay off a bit would ya?' the other guy berates.

'It's probably all those steroids causing him anger issues.' I start to pull myself up from the ground the best I can with ropes around my wrists. 'You do know that stuff does other things to men too, you know…' I bounce my eyes back and forth from Kyle's face to his crotch. His arm swings up to strike me again just as numero uno douchebag walks through the door.

'Kyle!' He snatches Kyle's hand mid-air with his left hand and almost knocks him back on his ass with a punch to the jaw with his right. 'What part of 'Don't lay a hand on her,' did you not understand?'

'But, Mr. Smith… You didn't hear what she said,' He says like a petulant child, rubbing his jaw which is already turning blue and purple.

He rubs his temples. 'You know what? Just get the fuck out of here and go make sure everything is set for the fight tonight.'

'I'm sorry, boss.' he mumbles as he makes his way out the door like a scolded child. Honestly, it's kinda sad for a grown man to be brought to his knees like that, but I can't help but smile inside, knowing he got what he deserved after the asshole smacked me.

'Get her off the floor and tie her to the chair. We don't need her running and for you dumbasses losing her again.' Goon number two doesn't say anything, just starts pulling me up from the filthy floor. 'Sorry I had to grab you again, Chloe, but the deal got thrown out the window and now I have to take a different approach to getting what's owed to me.' Mr Smith pulls a chair across the room, scratching against the floor, making me cringe.

'Where's Dom? And why do we have to go through all this again? I'm just gonna try to escape again like I did last time, this time I'll make sure I get further away. Maybe I'll just go back to America this time. Nothing you can do to hurt us if we're across the ocean, eh?' He places the chair down in front of me and takes a seat. The smug look on his face does nothing to take the edge off my nerves.

'Oh, Chloe. There are so many things wrong with everything you just said. Obviously, your father didn't tell you the type of man I am.' He runs his hands across the stubble of his chin and I can feel my stomach flop inside of me. But I don't want him to see my fear, so I reel it all back in, putting my tough girl mask back on.

'Where's Dom? I know he was here. Did you hurt him?'

'Calm your tits. I haven't seen Dom the Dominator. Quite honestly, he's the reason you're here this time.' He steeples his hairy hands together in front of him. 'I just talked with him a bit ago, he knows what he needs to do now. I own him.'

My tough girl mask slips and I can't help the tears that start to travel down my cheeks. What have I done? I should have left Dom and Nan out of this. I've ruined those kind people's lives.

'What do I need to do to help him? To get you to leave him be?' My voice breaks along with my heart.

'My money back with interest. That's all I want Chloe. That's all I've wanted this whole time.'

'My father said he doesn't have it. And there's no way he's able to come up with that much money. I don't how you expect us to come up with that much. Maybe if I talk to my dad, we can try to come up with some type of payment arrangement?' I plead with him.

'Chloe, Chloe, Chloe! That's what I was generous enough to do for Dom, and look how well that turned out.' He pulls a face like I should understand.

'But his grandma was in the hospital. You have to have some compassion in you. Please Mr. Smith!'

'Nope. Can't do it. And as for you being able to break free again, not happening. As you can see, this isn't my back office this time. It's secure and you'll not be going anywhere, my men and your ropes will ensure you don't. No one can get to you, so, get comfortable, sweetheart, you're gonna be here awhile.' He gets up, pushing his chair back to the desk, making that god-awful sound again, and he starts to head for the door. 'I'll talk to your dad again, maybe he'll come to his senses, pull his head out of his ass, and come save his only daughter.' With that he leaves. Goon number two is left behind, he deadbolts the door in three different spots and goes back to his post next to the door.

The tears flow freely from my eyes now and I don't give a crap if he sees me. Maybe it'll give him the impression I'm vulnerable and it'll help in my favour. For right now though, that's the furthest of my thoughts. Is Nan okay? Is Dominic alright? I've ruined their lives. How can I ever live with myself after this? This is not an oopsy I bumped into your car, let me pay for that. It's an oh my god they tried to kill your grandma and then forced you into working for them for the rest of your life, type of thing.

What do I do?

How do I save them when they're trying to save me?

Dom

I LOOK MR. Smith directly in the eyes as he smirks my way. 'I have a lot of money riding on this fight, Dom, do not lose.'

'I'll fucking win, but you're taking me to Chloe afterward.'

'Get in the fucking cage.'

I do reluctantly. I'm the first to enter. I haven't had a second to prepare myself like I normally would. But I'm still confident I can wipe the floor with the guy walking toward the cage. He's tall I'd say six foot six and he's built, pretty much matching me in muscle. I haven't seen this guy around before. A thought flits through my mind as I walk to the centre where the ref holds both our hands together as he chats his usual shit. Maybe this is a set-up, maybe this guy's a ringer, and he's got him in specifically in the hopes he'd beat me. Maybe he doesn't really want me to win, so he can have me over a barrel. Fucker, either way I'm winning, even if it kills me.

He show boats a little around the ring and looks toward the crowd left of the cage, right where Mr. Smith is sitting. Motherfucker. As he bounces on his toes stepping toward me I test his reflexes, with a quick jab, he's fast and he blocks with his elbow. The guy has game, but I'm better. I walk a few steps with my guard dropped giving him the perfect opportunity to take me down. He takes the bait and as he throws a right, I swing mine and clock him on the chin. He looks pissed but he's steady.

We play around like this for four rounds. I should have finished it in round two but I wanted to make Mr. Smith sweat. We've traded blows and right now it's a close call to anyone looking in, but only because I've let it be. See the guy now feels confident he can win, and Mr. Smith is worried as fuck not knowing who will win. Will he lose more money or win big? Who the fuck knows, but what I do know is I've been holding back. And when I finally let loose, he's not going to know what the fuck has hit him. Round six and I decide I've had enough play now. I want to see Chloe. I wait for the tell when he drops his shoulder. I know where he is going and what he's going to hit me with. Every damn time he throws a left he drops his right shoulder. I duck move forward and pound his body with blows, up against the cage he tries to push me off but I hold him trading blows from his solar plexus and kidneys. When he looks like he has nothing more to give I step back and give him a sporting chance. He raises his hands feebly trying to protect his face and body with his elbows. But it doesn't stop me. I side step, bringing up my leg in a roundhouse kick. Knocking him out cold.

I leave the ring and head straight to Mr. Smith. He has two men guarding him and they both square up to me. I'm bleeding and my eye is stinging like a bitch, but my adrenaline is pumping and I'd be more than happy to take on both right now.

'Sit the fuck down.' Mr. Smith tells them rolling his eyes. 'Dom, you did as you were told, good lad,' he says like he's talking to a fucking dog. I grind my teeth and tense my jaw.

'I want to see her. Now.'

'No.'

'Either take me to her or I'll ring the cops and have this whole fucking place shut down.'

He laughs like I just cracked the funniest joke in the world. 'Half the fuckers here are coppers, Dom, don't be an idiot.'

'I'm not fighting again until I see her.'

'Oh for fucks sake you have it bad eh? She got your balls real tight huh?' I don't give him the satisfaction of an answer. I just glare at him.

'Come on then, I suppose we can manage a conjugal visit. If you don't mind an audience while you fuck her?' He chuckles—he actually thinks he's funny.

'Go fuck yourself.' I tell him as he stands from his seat.

'Oh here I was thinking you wanted to see your little whore? Maybe I should go fuck her instead?'

'You touch her and I'll fucking kill you.' I growl and his bodyguards put their hands on me, blocking my view of him. He swats them away and walks through the gap.

'Come on, Dom, I'm feeling generous but don't push your luck.' I should strangle the fucker right here for what he did to my nan, but I need to know where he's keeping Chloe, I can't do jack shit until I know where she is. He leads me to a door through the back and we walk down what looks like an old maintenance corridor. All the pipes and shit run right down it. We walk to the bottom and come to another door. As we get through there I see a guard on the other side, he has a cache of weapons and CCTV monitors. I do a quick once over and try to memorise every camera position from the screens.

We pass through three more doors and up a flight of stairs before we stop at a locked door. Mr. Smith knocks three times and the locks sound on the other side. I listen as the metal grinds against metal as each bolt slides home. As the door opens, Mr. Smith turns to me and gets all up in my face. I can smell the liquor on his breath.

'You make a move, they'll shoot to kill. I'll dump her so no-one fucking finds her body, we clear?'

Gritting my teeth together and holding my tongue, I nod my head. As I walk in behind him, the first thing I notice is the bruise across her cheek. I inhale and hold my temper. Her eyes widen at seeing me and then tears stream down her face. My chest hurts from being so fucking helpless. I move to walk forward and the fucker guarding her steps in my way. I stand toe to toe with him.

'Call your fucking dog off.' I growl to Mr. Smith, not taking my eyes off the fucker in front of me.

'Grant, back up.' The man blocking my path sneers as he backs the fuck up, but I pay him no mind. Chloe has my full attention as everything else pales into insignificance as I cup her face in my bruised hands.

'I'm so fucking sorry, Chlo.'

'This isn't your fault, Dom, none of it. Just go and don't look back, get out while you can. Look after Nan.'

I frown as she spouts that shit. Like she believes I'll actually leave her here. That pisses me off for a second. But then I realise she's just cut up about it, she's talking shit trying to save us. I smile as she pleads with me.

'Chloe, I got this okay?' Her eyes widen as she realises I'm not going to run.

'Dom, you don't have to—'

'Stop, I'm not leaving you here, you're going home with me.' A cold, calculated laugh, sounds behind me and I know who it is. I close my eyes and tense my jaw so tight my teeth grind together.

'Dom... Dom... Dom, the girl is staying with me. I've been generous, you've seen her, now get the fuck out.'

I don't move. The guy giving me the evil eye when I entered, steps to my right side. He looks huge from my low kneeling position, but he's going down.

'Dom please... please, I'm begging you... just go.' Chloe cries in front of me. I move closer to her and kiss her on the cheek, whispering in her ear.

'I have to go now, but I'm not leaving you. I'll be back I swear, I got this Chlo.' I watch as she nods frantically trying to stop the tears. I kiss her gently on the lips, and then stand.

'Enough of the fucking waterworks woman, you're in good hands.' Mr. Smith leers like a fucking predator. Instinct takes over and I swing for him. But I'm closed down by two men either side of me. I take multiple hits to the ribs and face. I curl up as I hit the floor and protect my head. Chloe screams out as they land blow after blow. That's the last thing I hear before I'm out cold.

***

Chloe

'Dommmm!' My wrists burn as I pull against the ropes, trying to free them so I can get to him. I can't tell if he's breathing. 'Stop. Please! Leave him alone.' The fucker chuckles as my chair topples over and my head bashes into the wall.

'Stupid girl. You idiots should have known not to mess with me. And to swing on me...' A guttural laugh comes out of his nasty ass mouth and fuels me more to try to get to Dom. '...Big mistake.'

I wiggle my legs trying to get leverage to drag the chair across the floor, a foot lands on top of the chair and a heavy weight stops me from going any further.

'Please... leave him be. Please, I'll do whatever you want.' Tears stream down the corner of my eyes, making it hard for me to tell if Dom is breathing. 'Is he breathing? Did you kill him?' I gasp in between words, struggling to get them out.

'He's fine.' He states without even checking. 'Grant, take this fool out back to the alley. I'm sure he can get himself home from there.' My heart plummets with thoughts of him all alone back there, struggling to live.

'Please, can you at least call an ambulance.' I choke out as Grant grabs Dom by his legs and starts dragging him out the door. His head hits the door hinge and I can no longer hold back the sob that breaks free.

Mr. Smith turns and closes the door as the last bit of Dom clears it. 'Okay, now that's dealt with and Dom knows where we stand and what to do now, I'm going to need you to call your father. We need to know what his plans are for his daughter's future.' He pulls my chair from the ground and puts me back on four legs. 'Do you think you can do that for me, sweetheart?'

'Yes, I can call him.' I quickly agree and make the choice of not starting more problems by throwing his condescending endearment back in his face. I'm smart enough to know that this is not the time, and after what they just did to Dom? I actually fear for my life now. 'If you have a phone I can use, I'll call him right away. Maybe if you guys come to an agreement, you will let me go?'

'Yeah, uh huh. Let's just see what daddio has to say before we go jumping to shit. Give me your phone.' He demands and holds out his hand for the fucktard goon to give his phone over. 'What's the number?' he directs towards me and I rattle off my father's number to him. 'I'm gonna put it on speaker, don't try anything stupid. Remember what your boy toy looked like just now? Don't make stupid choices, ya hear?'

'Yes.' Pushing send, he sits the phone facing up on the table closest to my rickety wooden chair, and it immediately starts to ring.

'This is Mike, how can I help you.'

'Daddy…? It's Chloe.' Tears well up in my eyes at the sound of his voice.

'Chloe, where are you? Are you alright? Where are you calling from?' He rapid fires the questions before I have an opportunity to even answer one.

'Dad, I'm with Mr. Smith again. I can't say much right now, but he's wanting me to ask, what you plan on doing to save me, daddy?' My chest starts trembling as more sobs break loose. 'Dad, they hurt Dom, really bad. And I don't know if he's okay.' I glance up at Mr. Smith and the glower he has on his face tells me that I need to stay on topic. 'Dad?'

'I'm here Chloe. Is he there with you?'

'Um, Dom or Mr. Smith?'

'Yes, Patrick… Mr. Smith. Whatever he's choosing to go by now. If he's there, put him on the phone, baby.'

'I'm right here, Mike. But I figured you'd want to talk to your daughter and tell her how you're gonna fix this mess you've got her in.' He leans on the table, crossing his ankles, with a smug look on his face. He knows he's holding all the cards. If my father doesn't have a solution, I know for sure I'm not going home today.

'Patrick, just let her go. We can make some sort of an arrangement. You don't need her.' I can hear the pleading in my dad's voice.

'Dad, what are you going to do?'

'I'll take care of it honey, I promise.' He clears his throat. 'Pat, just let her go and you and I can work it out.'

'Nope that's not gonna work. I tried the whole work something out shit already, and so far all it's done is land your daughter right back in my lap. I will do this though, I'll give you a week to get me my money, or Imma start with her fingers. Maybe I'll even send you a video so you can hear her screams.' My heart plummets into my stomach at his words.

'Alright, alright, Patrick, I'll figure it out. Just give me the week.'

'One week, Mike. One week!'

CHAPTER THIRTEEN

Dom

I DO MY best to clean myself up in the bathroom, but I keep having to stop to hurl again. I think I have a serious concussion.

On any other day, I'd have taken my ass to the hospital to be checked over. But there are so many reasons why I can't do that. I need to figure out a way to save Chloe, be there for my nan and make plans with Andre. Not to mention the police asking questions if I turned up at the hospital like this.

My head is muzzy and I'm struggling to stay conscious. I don't even know how I got here, or what fucking day it is. Clearly, I'm not in a good way. I turn the shower on and over the din of the water running I hear the trill of my phone ringing. I stop, trying to pinpoint where the noise is coming from. I sway on my feet and stagger to my bedroom door. The noise stops momentarily but it starts up again just as quick. I look around swaying like a drunk and bend to lift my shorts from the floor. I don't remember taking them off. I look down and realise I am in-fact only in my boxers. The shorts are covered in blood. Deciding this is definitely where the noise is coming from, I fumble around trying and failing to get my hand in the pocket to retrieve the phone. I try again and my head spins at around the same time my stomach flips and I lose what little I had left in my stomach leaving me dry heaving on my hands and knees.

I hurt everywhere. I'm not sure if it's the thumping in my head, beating its own tune like the worst fucking hangover in history, or the pain in my ribs that hurts more. It could be a tie between the two. I dry heave again and groan as my head feels like it might implode. I crawl across the floor and the phone still ringing somewhere sounds further and further away as I feel myself slipping into unconsciousness.

***

I'm not sure if the noise I can hear is my blood pounding angrily around my head or it's coming from somewhere else as I open my eyes. I blink realising only one eye is working. I feel strange like I'm not inside my own body. What the fuck is wrong with me? I push up from the floor, realising the banging is coming from downstairs and groan as pain shoots through my chest. The banging is coming from the front door to be more precise. I get up only for the room to spin, steadying myself against the wall, I try to get myself in motion.

As I get to the top of the stairs someone shouts through the letterbox. 'Dominic it's Andre.' Every god damn step down the stairs pains me, and it takes at least five before I get a decent rhythm going and my feet get with the programme. I get to the door and find an angry guy, big about six feet and then some out on the front step. But as he takes me in, the anger seems to dissipate and concern etches his features.

'What happened?'

'I lost.'

'I saw you fight last night you didn't lose.'

'Last night?' What the fuck? 'What time is it?'

'It's almost lunch time, I've been calling your phone all morning.'

'Shit, wait…' I close my one functioning eye as the pain ramps up a notch and my brain tries to fight through the foggy events of last night. I don't like what I remember. My hands go out to grasp for the doorframe and Andre steps forward and holds me up.

'You need to lay down.' He holds me up and helps me to the living room. I fall onto the sofa and my head spins. Andre makes a phone call while I try to gather my thoughts and not throw up over Andre's shoes. I try leaning forward on my knees but the room spins and my head thumps the back of the sofa. Ouch. 'Fuuuck.' I try and listen to Andre's conversation but the thumping in my head takes precedence. And the rest is white noise.

I must pass out because when I'm hauled up and pulled to standing Andre slaps me around the face. 'Come on you're seeing the doc.'

'No… no, they'll call the police.'

'Not that kinda doc, I know a guy.'

I'm put in a car and taken... well, I'm not sure where. I lean my head against the glass and the motion of the car hurts my head. Jesus fucking Christ I'm a mess.

***

When I wake I have a drip attached to my arm. I sit up and expect the dizziness to take hold but it doesn't. Looking around I try to orientate myself. I'm in someone's bedroom. Looks a lot like my nans, there's frilly shit all over the place. Sitting up I find my feet and clamber up. The drip is attached to a stand which I roll along with me to the door. I open it and listen. I'm pretty sure I can hear someone down the stairs. I move slowly because I'm stiff, really stiff and not in a good way. It's the hit by a fucking freight train kind of stiff, not the I had a good workout kind. Pain radiates upward toward my head with every fucking step I take. I get to the top of the stairs and realise I can't go down with this stand. So I shout.

'Hello?'

Andre comes into sight and walks up the stairs, passing me and going into the room I just came from. I follow sitting back on the bed while Andre takes a seat in a pink flowery chair.

'Where are we?'

'A friend's house, she tended to you, checked you over and cleaned you up.'

'Well thanks. I guess I'm still a mess.' He nods not saying much else. 'I need to get Chloe and my nan is still in the hospital, do you have a phone?' He nods reaching into his pocket. I take it realising I don't have Zoe's number to memory.

'How long have I been here?' *Please only say one night* I look up the hospitals number and dial as he answers.

'Two days.'

'Fuck that long?'

'You were in a bad way. You had a severe concussion and you have broken ribs and some other things I don't remember the names for.'

'I'm supposed to fight every night, they have Chloe they took her.' I stop talking and hold my hand up as the phone is finally picked up at the other end. I explain when I'm put through to my Nan's ward who I am and why I'm calling. The nurse goes off and gets Zoe.

'Dom? where the fuck have you been?'

'Zoe I'm so fucking sorry, Chloe was taken and I was beat up real bad. I've only just come around a few minutes ago.'

'Oh my god, Dom what do you mean she was '*taken*', what the hell is going on with you? You're scaring me.'

'Zoe, I swear everything will be okay, I'm so sorry about everything, is my nan okay?'

'She's good Dom she should be able to go home sooner than expected, she's talking and eating really well.' Relief floods me at Zoe's words.

'Thank you, Zoe, so fucking much I don't know what I'd do without you.'

'Just get your ass here stat I need a damn shower I stink.' She laughs.

'Listen I'll get there as soon as I can, but I'm attached to a drip at the minute—'

'Are you serious? It was that bad? Oh god, Dom, I'll be here however long I'm needed just get better real quick! And keep in touch!'

'You're the best.' I sigh in relief knowing Nan is in good hands.

'I know there's stuff you're not telling me, but please tell me Chloe is okay?'

'She will be.' I tell her as honestly as I can. And just the thought of anything happening to Chloe guts me. I hang up the phone and Andre clears his throat. I look his way and hold out his phone.

'We need to discuss the business of Patrick Smith.'

'Yes, yes we fucking do.' This motherfucker has to die.

***
Chloe

'Get up, girl.' I'm jostled awake by someone kicking my leg. 'We're moving you today.' He says as he pulls me up off the floor by the bindings behind my back. Patrick popped his head in yesterday and told them to let me off the chair but to keep the ropes tied around my wrists. I thought maybe something was about to happen but after hours of sitting against the wall, my eyes finally drifted closed.

Dom's wellbeing is the last thought on my mind before sleep takes me and the first thing as I wake. I've been in this room for what I think is about a week. With no windows or a way to keep track of time, I just don't know. I tried to do that whole draw lines on the wall thing like you see in prison movies but after the third attempt of trying to do it behind my back, tied to a chair, I gave up. Especially when my nail broke half way down from trying, I could feel the blood dripping down my finger. Luckily none of the assholes were in here to see the tears roll down my cheeks from the pain. They would have loved that.

'Where are we going?' I ask hoping he'll give me an answer, already knowing that he probably won't. Anxiety settles in when I realize that Dom isn't going to know where I'm at anymore. 'Are we leaving the building? Isn't there still a day or two on the deadline Patrick gave my father? Where are you taking me? Dammit let go of me.' I struggle against the grip he has on my shoulder, but it does me no good. His nails dig into my skin and I shrink down from the pain. 'Please just tell me something.' I plead with him, not getting anywhere. He pushes me out the door and immediately turns right, heading in the direction of the exit sign. God please don't let them take me any further from Dom.

'Get out the door.' He nudges my back with his elbow and I barely catch myself from tripping over the door trim. My eyes immediately squeeze closed as the light from outside hits them. The sun is beating down, but once my eyes start to adjust, I focus and see a decked out black Bentley in front of me, right where the man is heading. The door pops open. As I try to cautiously peep inside, fucking goonface pushes me in and I land face down on the black cold leather.

'Owww.'

'Get the fuck in.' Is all he says in return. I adjust myself and try wiggling into the seat as best I can with my arms still restrained.

'How are you doing today, Chloe?' Looking over, I come face to face with Patrick Smith, number one asshole himself.

'Can you tell me where we're going? I thought you agreed a week with my dad?' I rapid fire the questions at him. Really hoping to get some answers. I learned the first time they took me that he's always the chattier of the bunch of kidnappers.

'Gotta move ya, toots. I did agree for a week, but we can't take no chances with keeping you there when Dom knows where it is. And since none of the people I sent to check on his whereabouts have been able to find him, I'm taking every precaution. Stupid guy hasn't even shown up for his fights, and he knows what happens if he doesn't.' He pulls a flask out of his pocket and takes a swig, returning it right where he got it from. 'Couldn't even find him in any hospital. I think he's bailed on you. I wouldn't blame him if he did. But he's a part of this now and he owes me now just as you and your father do.'

'Was he in your debt before I came along?' I question him while trying to think up ways to get Dom off the hook.

'Nope. He just showed up, fought his fights, which he always won. Took his money and left. Always predictable with him. He's been pretty consistent over the last few years. Brings in the big bucks for me too.'

'So, if he wants out, why don't you just let him out?'

'Cuz he stuck his nose in the wrong man's business and took something that didn't belong to him. No one crosses me and gets away with it.' Out comes the flask again, but this time he angles it towards me after he takes a drink, I shake my head no.

'So, it's all my fault? My dad's fault, that you're going after him and his family?'

'Yep, don't that just make you feel all warm and fuzzy on the inside. Your little fuckbuddy is involved 'cause he tried to help you.' He laughs out loud at himself. 'God lord almighty, I hope that was some good ass pussy he got in return.' He continues to laugh.

I have no response for his, my heart feels like it's breaking in a million pieces. I turn my head toward the window for the rest of the drive, trying to figure out where we're at. But it's pointless. I haven't explored London much since moving here, mostly have just stayed near my apartment. We pass an Italian restaurant named Gregorio's and I take note to try to at least remember it in case it comes in use. The vehicle starts to slow and I try to look around more, noticing where we could be. But as I stare out the window I'm entrenched into pure blackness. A bag of some sort of canvas material is pulled over my head.

'Is this necessary? You've not put it on the whole way here.' I enquire.

'Yes.' That's all he says. I hear the door pop open and I'm pulled down from the seat. I'm thrown over someone's shoulder and I can tell we're heading up some sort of steps. The atmosphere changes as we enter the place. Loud, swishing noises and people talking in a different language. I'm not sure but I think it's Chinese or Japanese. The sounds cease off in the distance and the man stops walking.

'Fuck.' I yell as I'm thrown down on my butt and the bag is roughly torn from my head, taking some of my hair with it. 'Do you need to be so damn rough?' I try to rub my head with my shoulder to soothe the ache of where my hair got pulled but after a minute I give up because there's no way I can reach it. Patrick opens the door and enters the room. I crane my head to see out of the door before it closes and there's lines of tables with men working at them, money counting machines in front of them.

'What is this place? A drug house?' My eyebrow raises at Patrick as he shakes his head at me.

'No, it's not a fucking drug house. What kinda man do you take me for?' I huff out a laugh at him but he continues without giving me the chance to respond. 'Just stay here a bit. Your dad has a couple more days to get back to me. Who knows, you could be outta here before you know it.'

Both the men exit the room, leaving me all alone. My hands are still bound behind my back but at least I'm not tied to a chair this time. Bright side, right? I send a silent prayer up to God, please let this nightmare end soon.

CHAPTER FOURTEEN

Dom

CHLOE WAS MOVED. Andre had tabs on them when I was laid up, but he lost them. I'm not a hundred percent yet, but I'm better than I was. My nan is coming home today and thankfully Zoe is bringing her back for me. I have a lot of explaining to do when she arrives because she's pissed. But my nan at least has been blissfully unaware which for once has worked in my favour.

I'm waiting for Andre to come back to me with more news, but so far they've come up empty. I know I have to go back and fight, otherwise I'll never find out where she is. I'm still black and blue, but my face is healing well and the swelling has all but gone now. I can see with both eyes luckily. I do have one eye a different colour to the other now though which is really weird. But the doc said its due to heavy trauma and it can happen. So what was once a dark brown colour is now blue. But it's functional and that's all that matters.

I think my hands were stamped on too. It's the only explanation for the mess they're in, I'm pretty sure most of my fingers were broken or dislocated. I flex them and then make a fist. It hurts but it's bearable. I try it a few more times hoping the pain in them will subside. But it doesn't it only gets worse. I was also pissing blood for three days, no doubt due to the battering my kidneys took. But I can't think about all this right now. I have a slew of fucking injuries and every single one of them means I'm not a safe bet in the ring. How can I go out to win if I'm halfway fucked up before I even get in there?

A knock on my front door gives me pause for a second. I answer finding Patrick himself smiling up at me like we're old friends. Fucker. I grind my teeth together and bite my tongue. Inviting him in with a sweep of my hand. He walks in front of me with his bodyguard at my back. As we get into the living room he sits down without being asked and puts his feet up on my nans coffee table. That irritates the fuck out of me and I knock his legs down. He doesn't say anything just grins a little harder.

'What do you want?' I bark out.

'Oh now, Dom, let's not start off like that. We're all friends here right?'

'The fuck we are asshole.'

'Always so vulgar.' He tsks and shakes his head like he's disgusted by my insult.

'FYI, Friends don't kidnap girlfriends or have them beaten up.'

'But we are just starting out at this relationship Dom. It's only just getting to a stage where I feel understood, am I understood Dom?' His voice is sickly sweet, like he's talking to someone's grandmother.

'Yeah I understand you. You're a sick, twisted motherfucker who gets his rocks off on hurting women.'

'I do believe you're not a woman, unless I am sorely mistaken, perhaps we should find out?' He nods to his bodyguard who steps up and tries to grab a hold of me. But I don't let him. As I swing he ducks and my timing is off because he lands a punch on my jaw. I see stars but quickly recover when the guy tries to yank at my sweat pants. Oh fuck no. I kick out grabbing the waistband, holding them tight. I kick again and his shin takes the brunt, but his hands come away from me and go to stopping him hitting the floor. I pull the cord tight and knot it so I'm not caught short again and I stand waiting for the next attack. Patrick chuckles behind me. I glare at him and he laughs harder still.

'Fucking coward, had to have me beaten by five men before you'll come talk to me.'

He laughs loudly and my blood starts to boil. Motherfucker.

'No, Dom, that beating was a lesson. One I hope you've learned? You don't get to touch me. Ever. And I own you. Remember that and it won't need to happen again. Now let's get down to business, because every night you don't turn up the more money you owe me.'

I sigh in resignation. Will this ride ever fucking end? 'Give me Chloe and I'll fight every fucking night as promised. You can't expect me to fight and win after the state you left me in. So, any money lost is on you not me *friend.*'

'Oh, Dom, another lesson you obviously need to learn is that I'm always in charge even when you think you are. I will always be here breathing down your neck. Oh, and the money lost just doubled. So, if I were you, I'd shut the fuck up.' He chastises me like I'm a child. Fucker. My teeth grind together and I bite my tongue. I will take so much pleasure in watching this bastard die. The thought eases my frustration a little.

'Fine you're in charge. Just please let Chloe go, what difference does it make to you if she's here? We can't go anywhere.'

'Oh but then where is your incentive?'

I shake my head. 'How about knowing she'll be taken if I don't? You've proven your point once. I won't step out of line.' I hear a car door as the last words leave my mouth and it's like everything goes into slow motion, as I watch through the window at my nan and Zoe walking up the path to the front door.

'Dom?' Zoe's voice echoes down the hall.

'Oh how nice to see you again.' Patrick smiles as they round the corner into the room. Zoe pales and almost takes a misstep. My nan smiles and offers her hand in greeting.

'My son has forgotten his manners,' She smiles. 'How nice to see you...Err?'

'Patrick, Ma'am.'

'Well how about a cup of tea?'

'Nan, Patrick was just leaving he's already had a drink.'

'Nonsense I can stay and have a cup with your nan, Dom, don't be rude.' Zoe looks at me her face a picture of fear. Patrick was the one who tried to smother my nan, I know that now. Nan takes her coat and scarf off and sits in her usual chair, while Patrick gets comfortable on the sofa end. Zoe is still stock still and looks like she's unable to move from shock. I snap my fingers in front of her face and she looks at me, her eyes welled up with tears. How the fuck do I deal with this shit without everyone getting hurt? And where the fuck is Andre?

***

Chloe

Is this how a caged animal feel? If so, I'm picketing all zoos and fighting for their release back into the wild. I can't be sure how long I've been here, but it seems like a lifetime. Staring at the same walls, day in and day out. Sleeping non-stop because there's not much else to do. I've even tried talking to the fuckers who are keeping me here when they come into take me to the restroom and give me food, but it's it always turns out to be a one-sided conversation no matter what craziness I throw at them. Patrick hasn't returned since the first day they brought me to my new living quarters. I've asked to speak with him, but my requests fall on deaf ears. So now I sit here lost in my own head, counting the cracks in the wall. There's fifty-three. I know for sure because this is my umpteenth time counting them.

No matter how much time has passed, my mind stills wanders back to Dom. I'm positive he followed my instructions and just let it be and moved on with his life. Taking care of Nan, finding a new way of supporting her, trying to right the disaster I've made of his life. I really don't blame him. Even if we had a mind-blowing connection and our bodies screamed out for one another, he has to think of what's best for Nan's health and his life. No matter if I die tomorrow, I'll never regret giving him a piece of me that no one else has ever had. I may even have given him a piece of my heart at the same time.

The rickety old door swings open and Kyle is here to take me to the bathroom, just like clockwork. Although I really wouldn't know because there's no clock in here, but it sure seems that way.

'Time for me to empty the canister, eh?' I pull myself up from the floor the best I can. 'What's on the menu for tonight? Please don't tell me it's peanut butter and jelly again. Can't we mix it up a little, maybe get me some Chinese takeout or damn, even something from the fast food drive through.'

'Shut up and move.' He throws my food down on the wooden table, pb&j as predicted, and puts the black canvas bag over my head.

'Oh, feeling a little talkative today, are we? It's about damn time. I think I was starting to get tired of my own damn voice.'

'I said shut up.' And with that he yanks the bag securely down and directs me to the bathroom. Long hall, right, right again, and then left into the bathroom. He nudges me in and yanks the bag from my head, slamming the door behind him. After doing this so many times, I've gotten used to the wiggle wiggle skooch skooch to get my pants down and back up. I used to get angry pounds on the door when I took too long, but fuck what do they expect. My damn hands are bound. I finish my business and do a shake to try and dry the piss from my crotch. If I ever get out of here, the first place I'm going is to the gyno to get myself checked. I know there's a UTI on the horizon.

I give two kicks to the door to signal that I'm done and Kyle pops in and begins to jam the bag back over my head. He has it down to my mouth when I feel the weight of his hands on the bag disappear. I hear a scuffle in the doorway and try to use my shoulder to get the bag up off my eyes to see what's happening. My body hits the wall as I lose my balance. Pushing my head against it, I manage to manoeuvre the bag up over my nose and get it so one eye is able to see out. I rush back over to the door and get there just as a man chokes out Kyle. I've never seen a man killed before and I'm frozen to the spot. Who is this man?

'Come on, we gotta go before anyone finds the body.' The mystery man grabs my arm after he pulls Kyle's body into the bathroom and closes the door.

'Who are you?' I question as he drags me down a back corridor and out a door where I'm met with blinding light, I run through the pain of the burn, seeing freedom on the other side.

'No time to explain now. Just know that your father sent me and that you can trust me.'

'My dad?'

'Yes, now come on. There's a van waiting on the other side of this building.' We both break into a full sprint down the back alley and around the corner. Thank God he kept a hold of my arm or I for sure would have been face down on the cement from my legs being so wobbly. 'Get in the back.' He tells me as we approach the van. 'I'll be right back.'

'Wait wait. Where's your phone? I have to call Dominic and let him know I'm okay.'

'He's in the building. Now get in the back and don't open the door for anyone but me.' I do as he says and climb in through the sliding door and lock it behind me. Dom is in the building. What's going on? Has he been taken? Is he fighting? Is he okay?

CHAPTER FIFTEEN

Dom

AS I GET to the meeting point, Andre comes into sight, his van behind him. I look at him waiting on him to say one way or another. *Please tell me you got her.* When he nods his head, I don't hesitate, my feet are in motion and I meet him halfway across the road. He turns and walks with me to the back of the van.

'Chloe open up.' He says quietly tapping, the adrenaline screams through my body and my heart races. It's been too fucking long since I saw her last, tied up and beaten. When the door opens, I don't even get the chance to speak because she leaps into my arms and wraps herself around me like a limpet. Sobs wrack through her body and she shakes uncontrollably in my arms.

'Hey, baby it's okay...it's okay you're safe now.'

'We need to move. Now.' Andre says into my ear.

I nod and holding Chloe tightly, I climb into the back of the van, sitting her so she straddles me chest to chest, I haven't even seen her face yet because she's been clung to me so tight. I pull my head back trying to see her. My heart breaks a little when I get a proper look. Her cheeks look sunken, she's lost weight, and she looks like she's been smacked around more than I care to imagine. I clench my jaw, my teeth grinding I try to hold the anger back. As the van jerks into motion she looks directly into my eyes.

'I thought... they... were going to... kill you.' She sobs the words out. 'Is... Nan... Okay?'

'Hey, hey stop. Don't cry, it's all going to be okay, I'm here now.' The van picks up speed and before I know it we're heading down a dark lane without the headlights on. Andre seems confident in his driving skills so I say nothing. When we come to a stop Chloe sits up and looks around, fear alive in her eyes. 'Listen you're safe now, okay? Chloe, look at me, I won't let anything happen to you again, okay?' Her head nods and she clings to me as Andre opens the back doors. I shuffle us to the end hop out, and carry her toward the small cottage which stands in darkness surrounded by the woodland around us. It's pretty damn beautiful even in just the moonlight. Andre flips the lights on as I get to the front door. Looking around I set her down on the sofa. Andre stands looking awkward in the corner. And Chloe looks suddenly worried.

'Where are we?'

'In a safe place, where they can't find us.'

'Us? Is Nan here? Zoe?' My heart drops a little as I swallow down the disappointment at what I had to do.

'No. Nan is in a care home right now, and Zoe is fine too. She's not happy with the situation but I did what I had to do to make everyone safe.'

'What you had to do?'

'My nan, I promised her she could live out her years at home.' I swallow down the lump in my throat. I had spent a lot of time online and visiting the homes while Chloe was held hostage. Because I knew this moment was coming. Zoe was obviously worried about Chloe but she didn't know the weight of the situation and still doesn't. So I didn't expect her to understand, she was angry over Nan, like really fucking angry. But gave me her blessing and told me that she loved me and that she knew I'd only do good by her. And she obviously wanted Chloe safe too.

'And she couldn't because of me?' Chloe says and tears swim in her eyes again.

'It's not your fault, please don't say that.'

'Can she come here?'

'No, she can't, she needs care that we can't give her like this.' I motion around us.

'I don't understand Dom, what do you mean?'

'Chloe, we didn't get Patrick. I fought yesterday and every day before that, until we found where you'd been taken. Patrick wasn't about to let me walk even if your dad paid the money. I was on the hook and he was going to fight me till it killed me. So it's not on you

Chloe, it's on him. My nan is oblivious to my promise and *we* needed out from under Patrick...so.' I shrug my shoulders.

'I wish you had never met me.' She sniffles. Well fuck that shit.

'Hey, listen up. I'm fucking glad I found you, and I won't have you thinking differently okay?'

'So much has happened and if you hadn't met me you wouldn't be in this mess.'

'And I wouldn't have you.'

She giggle hiccups and rests her head on my shoulder. 'I'm so sorry, Dom.' I hug her closer and look around the room at our little hideout. Its basic but from what I can see we'll be comfortable for a while. Andre clears his throat and I realise quickly I'd forgotten he was still here.

'So I stocked the kitchen you have enough to get by for the next couple weeks. You'll need to chop more wood for the fire but make sure to stay out of sight. There isn't any signal out here so we can't stay in contact. I will be down every three days. And I will keep you updated on your grandmother. I nod and stand as he walks toward the front door.

'Thank you for everything, Andre.' I pat him on the back.

'Just doing my job.' I wave goodbye and then it's just the two of us. I go over and sit back down looking Chloe in the eye she frowns and squints a little.

'Dom?'

'Yeah?'

'I know I've been gone a while but I'm sure you had two brown eyes when I left?'

***

Chloe

We spend the next few hours just sitting and getting caught up on everything that's happened since I was taken. Well pretty much he did all the talking because not much happened to me while I was gone, other than stare at a grimy wall twenty-four seven. My heart broke all over again as he told me about the aftermath of the fight between him and Patrick's lackeys. More like attempted murder in my mind. I can't say or do anything but cry all over again as the visual of him being dragged through the door flashes in my mind.

I don't know how long I've been curled up in his lap, but when I wake it's morning already. I gently climb off his knee so not to wake him and make my way to the bathroom. I had every intention of washing this filth from myself as soon as I could when we had arrived. But all the emotions and crying, happiness and joy of being saved, left me exhausted. I turn the knob on the shower and take a moment to take in all the cabin trim lining the bathroom. It's everywhere, but it was done tastefully. I take off my clothes and immediately throw them directly into the waste can next to the toilet. They don't all fit, but at this point I don't even care.

The water feels glorious as it cascades down my face and chest as I climb in the shower. I wash my hair not only once or twice but three times until I feel like it's clean enough. I suds up a washcloth and make to clean my body. Looking down, I see brown water making its way down the drain. How long did Dom say I was there? Three weeks? A month? I scrub my body repeatedly until my skin starts to feel raw and turns bright red. I still don't feel as if I'm clean enough, but it will have to do for now. I rinse myself, turn the shower back off, and grab the towel I'd seen hanging outside the curtain.

Wrapping myself up, I step out and almost end up right back on my ass on the floor of the shower tiles. Dom's arms wrap around me and catch me halfway, pulling me up against his bare chest. I can't help but to melt into him as his scent makes its way through my senses. I open my eyes and look up into his mismatched irises, there's no time wasted before his lips are on mine and I'm savouring the sweet taste of his mouth.

My towel drops and his hand comes up to cup my full breast, squeezing and rolling my nipple in between his fingertips. I moan into his mouth, but this isn't how I want our first time back together to go. He's done so much for me and I need to show him how much it means to me. I pull away from his kiss and bring my lips down his neck, suckling as I go down his chest. As I bring his nipple into my mouth, I push him back until his ass hits the sink behind him. His right hand flies to the countertop to brace himself, his left entangling in my wet hair. I release his nipple and continue my way down, counting his abs as I run my tongue down the defined ridges. Lowering a hand, I push his sleep shorts down till they pool at his feet and bring his cock up, rubbing my way up it as I go down. Settling on my knees, I run my tongue from the bottom to top of his shaft and wrap my lips around his head. His hand jerks in my hair. I have no intention of teasing this glorious man, my head starts to bob up and down as I bring him to the back of my throat and back up again. Reaching my hand up, I massage his balls as I hollow out my cheeks and take him further into my throat than I ever thought possible. His hand tightens in my hair as I look up, his eyes boring down at me, and I feel him losing control, his hips coming off of the counter as he starts to thrust into my mouth in response. His legs stiffen as he plunges into my mouth, my gag reflex barely hanging on as he jerks and empties himself down the back of my throat. Our breathing is ragged and I wipe my mouth with the towel laying on the floor next to me.

'That was…' I start to say right before his hands swoop underneath me and pulls me up, setting me down on the counter next to the sink. His lips reconnecting with mine, he gives his dick a couple of pumps before lining it up with my entrance.

'Dom! Chloe! Where are you guys?' Andre's voice booms through the little cabin. He sounds more worried than he did when I first met him.

'Be out in a second.' Dom yells back at him. He must have heard the same concern in Andre's voice because he pulls himself away quicker than I expect and once again I almost land on my ass. Luckily I catch myself at the last second. He tosses a t-shirt to me and jams his legs into his shorts before rushing out the door. I soon follow and find them in the living room, stood in front of the fireplace. I know it didn't take me that long to get out here but the look on Dom's face tells me he knows whatever bad news Andre came baring.

'What's going on? Please just tell me? Do they know where were we are?' I ask as I go into Dom's arms and turn to face Andre.

'Chloe, maybe we should take a seat.' Dom says to me as he attempts to pull me towards the sofa.

'No Dom, I'm not taking a seat. Please, just tell me what's going on? Why are you back so quickly Andre?' Dom's arms wrap back around me.

'Chloe, honey. It's Zoe.' Dom answers.

Dom

'WHAT HAPPENED? WHERE is she?' Andre looks to me and I nod trying to tell him I'll deal with whatever comes. Chloe's eyes are already filling with tears and just seeing her like this breaks my fucking heart.

'Andre found her this morning.'

'Found her? What do you mean *Found*?'

'She's dead.' I close my eyes tight as I feel her collapse into my arms.

'No... No...no?' Her head shakes violently back and forth against my chest.

'Was it them?' She turns looking at Andre, who nods his head. He doesn't say anything more and I'm glad because I want to spare her the details. Zoe was one of my only friends. The shock of Andre's news hasn't penetrated yet. And at the moment I'm glad because I need to be strong for Chloe. I need to make sure she's alright. I don't even know the extent of what she's been through yet, and there I am like a selfish bastard in the bathroom having her blow me.

'What about Nan?' Chloe asks her voice barely a whisper.

'I have men there round the clock she's fine,' Andre assures her.

Chloe exhales a breath. Relief I think. But as her shoulders shake and she hides her face, I know she's breaking right in-front of me.

'I'm really sorry.' Andre pats her shoulder and meets my eyes. 'I didn't honestly think she would be a target.'

'It's not your fault, Andre I should have known.' I grit my teeth together knowing I made a huge mistake not protecting her. They would have known how close she was to us from their time watching us in the hospital and when they came to my house. It was a stupid thing to do, and Zoe paid the price for my stupidity. Chloe takes herself off to the bathroom and I give her some space. I see Andre to the door. As he leaves, he stops, turning to me.

'You couldn't have known either.' I nod not saying a word. My guilt must be showing like a coat of armour. I can't shake it. As I watch him leave the drive, I close the door and sit at the small table in the kitchen. Resting my head in my hands, I let the enormity of Andre's news sink in like lead weight in my stomach. The internal battle inside of me is telling me I should mourn. But there is something else there too. Anger. Hate. Guilt. Those are the emotions that win out. And before I lose myself to the same place that Chloe is, I walk out of the front door. I find the Axe that Andre had used to chop wood and I take my anger out on the nearest tree. Zoe had been tied up and tortured. Andre thinks they may have raped her too. He found her face down in a bucket of water. And they killed her in my kitchen. I don't know why she was there but she had a key. He had taken care of her body and all the evidence. Not calling the police because I would be a suspect. THE suspect. As I chop the final piece, I look at the sun in the sky. It's moved, it must be at least eleven now. I head back into the cabin and find Chloe curled up on the sofa. Her face is tear streaked and her hair a mess like she's been pulling at it, from all angles. I realise that she has let it dry before brushing it. But I don't say anything. I sit in the chair opposite her. Not able to bring myself to enjoy her closeness. I don't deserve it.

'You okay?' I ask. Not saying a word, she nods in answer. I don't really know what else to say, so like a chump I don't say nothing.

'Do you hate me?' she asks in a quivering voice.

'What?'

'I understand if you do. God, I hate me, your life is ruined… because… of me.' She chokes back a sob. I frown and close my eyes on an exhale.

'Chloe, I don't hate you, why would you think that? Don't say shit like that, okay?'

'Why not? It's true.'

'It's not true, that's bullshit. Zoe is on *me*.'

'All of this is my fault, Dom, everything that has happened since I came into your life is my fault. You should never have helped me.'

She starts to cry uncontrollably and the guilt and anger I feel subsides for a moment while I pull her into my arms and hold her close.

'Hey shh.' I sway her from side to side like you would a child as you rock them, trying to lull them into a sleep. The pain tearing her apart radiates from her, and I don't know what I can do to make it better. I just hold her tighter.

'Babe, you haven't done anything wrong, none of this is your fault.' Her eyes meet mine.

'You don't believe that.'

'Yes, I fucking do, Chloe.' I allow a little of that anger to seep through. 'You didn't cause any of this, and you sure as shit didn't ask for it.' Her eyes widen at my certainty and she looks at her feet. Now I feel fucking bad for yelling at her. But she is beating herself up over something she had no power over. 'I don't even think your dad is either, from what we talked about, Patrick is a fucking lunatic and when things don't go his way he finds people to blame, he plays mind games and fucks with people's lives. He is the only one to blame here.'

'I thought you must hate me. Your nan in a home, and poor Zoe, oh god, Dom I can't believe she's gone.'

'Me either Chlo, but that bastard will pay for it I promise you that.'

***

Chloe

The days have just dragged by, it seems worse right now than it did when I was held captive. They say time heals all wounds, but it seems like every day that goes by, the pain of Zoe's murder hurts and haunts me even more. Andre has stopped by every other day to update Dom on his progress on finding Patrick. When he was here earlier, he said he's got a lock on his location, him and Dom are supposed to head out at dusk tomorrow.

'I just don't know why you can't let Andre handle it himself, Dom.' My silverware clashes as I slam my fork down on my plate. I try to reel in my anger, but the fear of something happening to Dom is too strong. I never intended on falling in love with this man, but I have and I don't want to lose him too.

'Chlo, I have to go. Zoe was my best friend, someone I counted on and held dear. I need to see her murderer brought down.' He leans back in his chair and I watch as his chest rises and falls. 'I have to Chloe, I just have to.' Leaving the table, he heads toward the bedroom.

I know he's hurting and trying to stay strong for me, but he also needs to grieve.

In that moment, I decide that I need to be there for him, just as he has for me. To be his shoulder, to be strong for him. I follow down the hall and give the bedroom door a gentle knock before opening it and making my way in. He's lying on the bed, propped up against the headboard. This man is the most beautiful I've ever seen and my pull to him is overwhelming. Even if I tried, the attraction I feel towards him is like a chemical reactor, no matter what situation we're thrown in. I climb up the bed and up his body, till my chin is resting on his chest, looking up at him.

'I'm sorry, Dominic. I know Zoe meant a lot to you.' His hands reach down, latching under my armpits, pulling me up to him. His arms tighten around me, his head resting in the crook of my neck. 'I'm so sorry, Dom, I'm so fucking sorry.' I feel his body shake under me as he silently cries, mourning the loss of his best friend. Tears trail down my cheeks as I stroke the back of his head, trying my best to console him.

There's a knock at the cabin door and I pull myself up from Dom. 'I'll get it, it's probably just Andre to get ready for tonight.' He puts up no argument, so I continue on my way out of the bedroom to the front door. Looking through the peephole, I see that it isn't Andre at all.

'Dad.' My voice screeches as I throw the door open. I can't catch myself before my hand flies away from me and the resounding smack of my fingers across his face echoes through the foyer of the cabin. His head snaps back towards me, an angry expression passing on his face quickly before realisation strikes.

'I'm sorry, Chloe. I deserved that.' He pulls me in for a hug and I don't resist. 'Can I come in?'

'Yeah.' Pulling out of his embrace, I back away from the entrance to make room for him to enter. Dom comes in to the kitchen, immediately extending his hand to my father.

'It's nice to meet you, Mr. Richards, I'm Dominic. Did Andre come with you?'

'No, he told me where to find you so I made my way here as soon as my plane landed.'

'Have a seat. You want a beer or water?' Dom asks while going to the fridge. I have no clue why he's being so nice to my dad after all he's caused, it's putting me even more on edge. I don't like it and I want to hit both their heads together.

'A beer would be nice thank you.' He replies as he makes his way over to the sofa. I follow and take a seat at the other end away from him and glare in his direction. I can't believe that he's here. I'm happy to see him safe but I want to punch him in the face as look at him.

'Is everything taken care of?' I snap but don't give him a chance to answer before I continue, 'What type of investment would cause someone to lose fucking millions? I need you to start from the beginning and don't you dare leave a fucking thing out!'

'Okay I'll start from the beginning, but you have to promise me you won't think any less of me.'

I scoff and close my eyes, biting my tongue against what I really want to say, 'That boat has already sailed. Now just tell me?'

CHAPTER SEVENTEEN

Dom

I SIT OPPOSITE Chloe and Mr Richards. Chloe looks uncomfortable and I question whether I should leave them alone. The resounding 'No,' I get from her has me staying in my seat though.

'You okay?' I ask her.

'Mm.' She nods and her father awkwardly starts to tell us how he's associated with Patrick fucking Smith.

'It's a short story really and not a lot to tell.' He pauses while he takes a sip of his beer. 'He was in a lot of gambling circles when he was in the States.' He shuffles in his seat like he's uncomfortable 'He moved around from state to state and obviously I came across him more than a few times. He's an arrogant bastard and he got himself in a lot of skirmishes, with a lot of bad people.' He wipes his brow and takes a gulp of his beer. 'He won big one night and asked me what he should do with his money. I told him to quit while he was ahead and pay his dues to whoever he owed.' He shrugs his shoulders and continues 'He didn't like that idea so I suggested he invest it, make more off it that way but, he would still be in debt. He liked the sound of that and I left him having won myself that night and thought nothing more of it.' Another gulp of his beer. 'A few months later word on the street was he was coming for me on account of that bad advice.'

'So you didn't steal his money?' Chloe asks.

'No, I'm not a thief, Chloe.'

'And that's what brought about him kidnapping Chloe?' I ask.

'Yes, he lives here, but like I said I never expected any of this to affect Chloe.'

Chloe looks like she's in pain.

'Hey, sweetheart you okay?' I cup her face and look her in the eyes. Nodding she shifts a little in her seat.

'I think I need to lay down.'

'I think you're right, come on.' I lift her into my arms and walk her to the bedroom, laying her down, while her dad stares from the open door. 'I'll be right back with some water okay?' I pass him in the doorway, he says nothing but looks at me strange. I fill a glass and get some ice from the freezer making sure it'll stay cold for her. As I get back, he's sat on the edge of the bed stroking her hair. I'm not sure how I feel about that so I push whatever the fuck that is back down and place the glass on the nightstand by the bed. I kiss Chloe on the head and motion for him to follow me out into the other room. He does without any hesitation and I close the door as he passes and follow him down the hall back to the kitchen.

'You want another drink?'

'Yeah why not, thanks.' As I take the lids off of two bottles of beer and hand him one, I watch as his hands shake slightly.

'Okay, so how about we cut the bullshit and you tell me what really happened.' He looks at me like he might lose his temper for a split second but then dials it back.

'What are you talking about?'

'I know damn well you just fucking lied to her face. I'm not an idiot, no-one travels across the world to fuck with someone's family over bad advice. How much did you take from him?' He has the audacity to look hurt over my questions.

'It's not what you think, I didn't steal his money.'

'So what did you do?' He takes a deep breath and closes his eyes when he exhales.

'I fell in love with his daughter.' That is not at all what I was expecting. Not. At. All.

'His daughter? Wait he has to be younger than you? How old is his daughter and please tell me she's a fucking adult?' I cringe when the words leave my mouth because if he doesn't give me the answer I want I might kill him myself.

'Of course, she's a fucking adult. What do you take me for?'

'How old is she?'

'Nineteen,' he mumbles as he starts picking at the label on his bottle.

'You're a fucking idiot, not to mention perverted, how fucking *old* are you?' I ask him, annoyed. Now don't get me wrong, by nineteen I was sexually active, and so are most girls that age *BUT* it's usually with guys of a similar age, not double that and then some.

'It doesn't matter because I love her.'

'You sound like a fucking teenager, Mike. She's younger than your own daughter!'

'They marry them off from the age of fourteen anyway.' He thinks that excuses him. They're gypsies. So not only has she gone off with a man almost triple her age but she's had sex before marriage and with a guy who isn't a gypsy traveller. No wonder Patrick is pissed. They disown their kids for less.

'So my best friend died because you couldn't keep it in your pants.' I growl. 'And you're in love with this girl and hoping your daughter won't find out?'

He nods. 'I don't want her to judge me for it.'

'Too late.' A voice comes from behind. Chloe dashes down the corridor to our bedroom, and I shake my head at him in disgust.

***

Chloe

I go into the bedroom and slam the door shut, following it with a punch to the white wall next to it. Pain radiates through my hand, but right now I don't even care. I can hear Dom yelling at my dad down the hall but the anger raging in my head isn't allowing me to hear what's actually being said. I'm so fucking mad. How dare he put me in this situation over a fucking teenage girl. That's gross and I'm beyond ashamed of him. I don't blame Patrick for going after me but at the same time, he should have just dealt with him one on one. There was no need for anyone to get hurt, especially murdered.

'Chloe, unlock the door.' Mike—yes, right now he's only Mike to me—says through the door. I know I shouldn't open it and let myself calm before having this confrontation but I'm just too pissed to wait.

Swinging the door open I hiss, 'What the fuck do you want?'

'Can we please just talk Chloe?' His eyes plead for forgiveness.

'What the fuck could you possibly say? That you made the decision to screw a girl that's younger than your own daughter and you're surprised when her father targeted you, you really didn't expect that *DAD*?' I'm so mad that I can't help the spittle that flies from my mouth as I yell at him. 'What would you have done if the situation was reversed, *DAD*? You going to tell me that you would have been okay with a fifty-eight year old man boning me?'

'Calm down, Chloe. You don't understand. I love Charity. I can't help that and there's nothing that can be done to change that. You know I've not let anyone in since your mom passed and then she came walking into my life and I just knew. We were meant for each other.' My stomach churns as his words hit. Is he fucking for real right now? Has he lost his ever-loving mind. Bile rises in my chest and before another word can be said, I make a beeline towards the bathroom and lose what little bit of food I had in my stomach.

'Get out and don't fucking come back until Chloe says otherwise.' The front door slams. I rest my head in my hands. 'Honey are you okay?'

'I don't know where that came from. I'm sorry.'

'You have nothing to be sorry for, love. You did nothing wrong and you had every right to say all those things.'

'No Dom, I'm sorry that Zoe's gone for these reasons. It was bad enough to begin with, but his reasons make it even worse.' I gasp trying to bring air into my lungs before continuing. 'He ruined all our lives.'

'One thing good came from all of this, babe. We found each other.' He turns me and wraps me in his arms. 'We'll get through this, Chloe, I promise.'

'Dominic, I…' Just as I'm about to tell him I love him, my stomach flips again and I turn and dry heave into the toilet, although I have nothing left to bring up.

'Come on, I have a glass of water in the room. I think you need to lay still a bit longer.'

I straighten up and he follows behind as I head back into bed. 'I don't know what's wrong with me, it must just be everything going on.' Dom pulls the sheet up over me and sits on the side of the bed. 'I really am sickened by everything that's happened. What should we do, Dom?'

'Andre should be here soon…'

'You're still going through with your plans?'

'Yes, Chloe. He's still out there coming after us. This has gone too far and it needs to end.' His thumb caresses my cheek as he brushes a piece of my hair behind my ear.

'But now that my dad is here, can't he just handle it?' I question.

'It's still going to be the same outcome, Chloe. Your father made it perfectly that he's not going to stop seeing Charity.'

'Do you think Andre knows the whole situation?'

'I'm going to assume so, babe. Andre is your dad's man, not mine.' Reaching over he grabs the glass of water off of the night stand and takes a sip before handing it to me.

'I know I'm pissed at him right now, but I should at least talk to him again before you guys head out, don't you think?'

'You can do whatever you'd like, babe, but I'm leaving with Andre when he gets here later. This really does need to end and I need to get Nan out of that care home.' He unknowingly begins to rub the Chinese script of his nan's name on his forearm.

'How can I get a hold of him?'

'Andre or your dad?' His brow quirks in question.

'Mike, my dad.'

'You may want to check in the driveway.' Leaning up, he pulls the string on the blinds until he can see to the outside. 'Yep, I was right. I never heard a car pull out.'

'Okay, I'm going to go brush my teeth and then talk to him.' I hop up off the bed leaving Dom still sitting on the edge. I'm determined to try to fix what I can. Or at least force my dad to fix this fucked up mess he's put us in.

CHAPTER EIGHTEEN

Dom

I GO OUT to tell Mike to wait up, he nods but doesn't get out of his car. I decide to make coffee, I don't really know what else to do. The whole situation is fucked up. I'm still not sure what I believe.

Why Patrick tell us it was over money and not his daughter? It just doesn't make sense to me. Surely the revenge wouldn't have been monetary? But regardless of the reason, Chloe and me are stuck in the middle of something we shouldn't be and I need to get it sorted no matter who is at fault. I can't forget what's happened. My nan... my best friend... and now we're stuck in hiding.

Patrick has to die.

I don't want us to be looking over our shoulder forever. I'm just about to pour the coffee when Chloe comes through the kitchen and opens the door to beckon her father back inside. A minute later and she's turning her back on him as he comes through the door. Pulling a chair out for herself she sits at the table and folds her arms across her chest. She means fucking business its written all over her face.

'Chloe—' Mike starts but she puts her hand up cutting him off.

'No, I want you to listen to me first.' She stops and glares at him for a moment and he shifts uncomfortably in his seat. 'On what planet is it normal for a man of your age to have sex with a girl of nineteen?' she asks, her fierce expression demanding an answer. He looks at his hands and starts to say something but changes his mind.

'It's not normal, Dad that's the answer, you're sticking it to a girl younger than your own daughter'

'Chloe—' I try and calm her down. But she puts her hand up again and glares my way, and my efforts go back to the coffee instead. As I watch Mike squirm in his seat. I almost smile at the way Chloe is handling him. Fuck she's hot like this. All bossy and mad as fuck. My balls almost jumped into her purse when she cut me off with that look in her eye. I leave the two cups I poured for them and sip my own leaning up against the counter, crossing my feet as I watch it play out in front of me. I'm amused but the situation isn't fucking funny. Not at all.

'How long have you been seeing her Dad? And why? How did that even happen?'

'It's a long story.'

'Well guess what *Dad* we've got nothing but time,' Chloe grits out through clenched teeth and then sits back in her chair. He huffs out a breath and wipes his brow with his hand. I take that opportunity to hand out their coffee. Chloe's eyes brighten a little as they meet mine and I smile as she takes the mug from me. Sliding Mikes in front of him he asks for sugar. I bring it back to the table and am just about to go back to my spot at the counter when Chloe grabs my hand as I pass and asks me to sit.

'Maybe we should talk alone, Chloe?' Mike pleads like he doesn't want to air his dirty laundry in-front of me.

'Are you kidding me right now? How dare you, his best friend was murdered, his nan was attacked and he's in hiding because of what you did so don't you dare even think about him going anywhere.' Chloe tells him how it is and I don't need to say a word. I relax back in the chair, fold my arms, and grin my best at Mike, proud as fuck of my girl. He huffs again and rubs his hands over his face.

'Okay, but it's not a pretty story and not something I would normally involve you in, Chloe.'

I laugh at his words. Too late for that.

'I buy and sell... some things... and there was a lot of trouble at one of the collection points and she was there, things got out of hand and she ended up being brought to me.'

'So you kidnapped her?' I ask before he can carry on. He has the decency to look embarrassed.

'Oh my god she has Stockholm syndrome,' Chloe says

'It wasn't like that.'

'Of course it wasn't.' She scoffs. 'Oh don't stop there, Dad, carry on.' She motions with her hand for him to hurry up. I almost snigger but it's not appropriate, so I hold it back. Just seeing her like this though is a turn on to say the least.

'So she was brought to me and we spent a lot of time talking and getting to know one another.'

'But she wasn't allowed to leave?'

'Well… she didn't want to leave.'

He's trying hard I'll give him that. He's making himself out like a fucking hero here.

'So it was instant attraction?' I ask with raised eyebrows.

'Well she didn't want to leave because what waited for her was a worse fate than me.'

'Oh so you rescued her?' Annoyance flits across his face as his daughter's sarcasm sinks in.

'She was being married off to a man from a family who was paying Patrick a lot of money so they could join the families through marriage. The Smith's are a big family that people don't fuck with.'

'Except you.' I point out. 'You had no problem fucking him over.'

'Look, I don't have to explain my actions to either of you, you have no fucking idea what it's like to live that life. I made sure you never had too.' He points at Chloe and his tone pisses me off.

'Watch yourself.' I growl as Chloe looks on indignantly.

'You can't excuse yourself so you get nasty, well it won't work with me, Dad.'

'You're right you don't *have* to explain yourself, but you fucking owe it to Chloe, fuck, you owe me an explanation after everything we've fucking been through as a direct result of *your* actions.'

'Look a lot of money was changing hands, Patrick was going to be a very rich man, all he had to do was give his daughter up to a fucking animal. He didn't hesitate. He agreed on the date and time and that was that, he didn't give a fuck about what she wanted, it was a business deal.'

***

Chloe

I take a deep breath in and try to calm myself. My nerves are wrecked and I know he probably deserves everything I say to him, but this isn't the time. Right now, our main focus is getting out of this mess, and whether I like it or not, Dom and I are a part of this now and there's no getting away from it.

'Alright dad, I get it. Right now, we need to deal with what's on the table and figure out how to get our lives back.' Dom's hand comes to rest on my thigh under the table and gives a light reassuring squeeze. This man has become my rock, and I love him even more for it. 'We can come back to the fact your screwing a teenager later.'

'Geez, Chloe, it's more than that.'

'Save it, it's no longer the time for that. Andre should be here soon and whether you like it or not, I'm being included in the planning on what happens going forward. Got it?' I look to both men, both scowling but they nod their heads in agreement knowing I won't budge on this. 'So, I think we can all agree that we can't just give Charity to them, it's just too dangerous. But we also cannot continue to live like refugees. Any suggestions?'

'Kill him.' Both men say at the same time. My eyes bounce back and forth between them and the expression on their faces tells me they're being serious.

'Um so we're just going to add murderers to our lists of crazy ass things we've done in our lifetimes?' I let out an exasperated laugh, truly hoping at least one of them come to their senses. But one glance between the two of them again tells me that that's not going to happen. 'Guys come on, we can't kill him.'

'What other options do we have, Chlo?' Dom's hand leaves my thigh as he turns to me, sincerity and determination in his eyes.

'I refuse to give her over sweetheart, and Patrick isn't going to stop until he has us all six feet under. So we may as well put him there first.'

'First, don't sweetheart me. Second, where is Charity and what are her thoughts on this? I know she's just a kid, but shouldn't she have a say?'

'She trusts me to do what needs to be done.' Andre chooses that moment to come walking through the door, his permanent 'I'm a badass, don't fuck with me look' plastered on his face. He's lugging two huge duffle bags and drops one down on the table in front of Dom.

'Let's get ready, Dom. We don't have much time before he moves again.' He starts unzipping the duffle and taking out gun after gun, 'and word on the street is he has something big in the works, so we need to move now.'

'I'm coming.' My dad stands up and starts to load a pistol.

'Wait… What?' My chair scrapes the hardwood as I jump up from my seat. 'Aren't we in the middle of trying to find other ways?'

'I don't know what you're talking about, but this has been the plan since I arrived and honestly we don't have time to fuck around right now. Whoever's coming, load up and get ready, we head out in fifteen.' Andre pulls the other bag from the table and heads off towards the spare bedroom.

'Dom come on. You can't do this.'

'We need to be prepared for whatever could happen, Chlo. We can't let this go on, you're in danger and I'm not okay with that. One way or another, this is going to end.' He tucks a gun in the back of his jeans and leans over, bringing me in for a kiss. 'We have to get our lives back.'

I try to protest the best I can but no one will hear me out. The love of my life is about to go to battle for me and he doesn't even know how I feel about him.

Fifteen minutes have passed and they all gather in the kitchen to finalize their plans. I can't listen and I angrily swipe at the tears that fall from my eyes. This may be the last time I see them and I'm to wait here not knowing what's happening and no phone. I'm sat in the living room and my dad pops in to say bye followed by Dom.

'Please promise to come back to me.' I beg of him and he pulls me up into his arms.

'I'll be back, Chloe, even if it's the last thing I do.'

'Dom?' His lips brush against mine and I look up into his multi-coloured eyes.

'Yes, baby?'

'I love you.' His mouth crushes into mine, showing me his feeling in one movement. Andre calls from the foyer and he let's go of me, kissing me on the forehead. No more words are said, and then they're gone.

CHAPTER NINETEEN

Dom

IF I SAID I wasn't scared I'd be lying, but right now as I walk away with Chloe's fuck up of a dad all I can think about are those words. And the fact I didn't say it back. I should have. But I have every intention of coming back and showing her just how much I fucking love her. My heart is pounding in my chest and adrenaline pumping through my veins. I've never gone out of my way to hurt anyone outside of the cage. But it's just like in the cage, either them or me. Do or die. I need to get in and out and make sure we all make it back. Fuck if I'm living in fear every time she leaves the house. I can't live like that and Chloe isn't going to either. And that's what I need to keep in mind when we get to where we're going. Do or die.

Andre is driving the van and I'm in the back, opposite me is Mike who he looks as cool as a cucumber and not in the slightest bit scared.

'You good?' he asks as he cocks his hand gun. I nod not saying a word. 'Fear is normal,' he says. 'On your first time.' Like killing people is an everyday occurrence for him. Maybe it is? What the fuck do I know.

'I'm fine,' I reassure him.

'Don't think about it just squeeze the trigger, you think about it you'll be dead in a second, they won't hesitate.'

I nod. 'Got it, hesitate you die.' He looks at me and a look of pride crosses his face. As the van comes to a stop Andre tosses some stuff over the seats to us and I watch as each of them pull on a balaclava and I do the same zipping my jacket up so my neck isn't on show and pull on black gloves which Andre gives me.

'Keep covered at all times, even though we will leave no witnesses, you can't have your artwork on show. Andre tells me, like a teacher talking to a student. Again, I nod. Apparently, Andre has men on all sides of the property we're going into. That makes me feel better knowing we have back up and it's not just the three of us.

As we move closer I get myself into the same headspace as I do before a fight. Focused no distractions. We get to the side door and gunshots ring out. Shit. Andre pushes me up against the side of the building and shots fire out all over the place. They know we're here. Fuck, bang goes the surprise. The shots are coming from the back and not being fired at us. So looks like Andre's men have been spotted. He does some shit with his hands which I'm pretty sure it means stay alert and follow me. But I can't be sure.

We creep along the wall and under a window. I stand at one side Andre the other and he mouths counting to three and in sync we cover the window, no one's there so we move along until we get to the side door. I turn and realise Mike isn't behind me. Where the fuck did he go? I scan the area but trying to see in the dark with no lights not even the moon, is like wading through quick setting concrete. Andre kicks the door open after another three counts and we move like we've done this a thousand times before. Watching each other's back's we clear the first room and each room we clear we get closer to the gunfire.

Now or never, Dom. Do or fucking Die. The door swings open and we open fire until we get to an alcove, where we duck in and I finally remember to breath. Not sure if I hit any targets, but sure as shit I tried. I take a deep breath and on Andre's count we duck out and fire again. This time I watch as a bullet connects with a guy in a shirt ugly enough it doesn't show the blood seeping through. He hits the ground, his gun aimed on us. He fires and everything seems to slow down. As I watch the bullet fly toward its intended target. Me. Andre knocks me out of the way and fires another shot killing the man on the floor. Fuck. I move in behind him and check no-one is coming up from the rear.

We make it to the end of the corridor with little problem and take out another two men through the last door. Realising from the sound of gunfire that more is going down outside the property than inside, we make our way to the back door. Andre opens it just a crack, looks out and then closes it again. He points to the stairs. We need to go up. We do, again in sync, guns cocked and ready to fire.

The layout upstairs is pretty much the same as down and we make our way down the corridor clearing each room as we go. All empty, but as we get to the final two rooms I can hear there are men inside. I twist the handle and Andre goes in first taking out two men as I fire on the third. I hit him directly in the chest and watch as the blood seeps through his clothes, and his eyes glaze over as his last breath leaves him. I don't have a chance to think about it, or feel anything, because Andre is moving onto the last room, as he opens the door this time I fire first and take out a man firing through the window out back. The force of the shot has him falling through the window. The guy beside him realises too late as Andre's bullet takes him out. Straight through the middle of his forehead.

With the room clear we move to the window as the shooting stops outside. Andre waves to his men and we move down and out the back door.

'Anyone have eyes on Patrick?' he asks. There is no answer. Fuck. This was a big waste of fucking time. I can't believe it. I bend at the waist and rip the balaclava off trying to catch my breath with my hands on my knees. My throat is red hot and I can't seem to get the air in fast enough. And for what? He wasn't even here.

'Where's Mike?' Andre asks looking around but we don't see him. 'Spread out, find him.' Everyone fans out and I get a really bad fucking feeling. Andre pulls me with him. 'He'll be fine.' He must have seen the look on my face. I go with him through the house, room by room, but we don't find him. Having seen him last outside, before we even got into the house we retrace our steps and eventually come across him in a clearing, flat on his back. Bleeding out.

***

Chloe

Just stay back and wait, Chloe. We'll be back in no time, they said. Don't worry, they said. I've been pacing this fucking cabin for the past 3 hours, not hearing a peep from any of them. I tried the whole, 'Don't worry' shit, but that lasted the couple of minutes it took me to get undressed to get into the shower. Which turned into not having a shower and throwing my clothes right back on. The man I love and my dad—no matter how upset I am with him, he's still my father—they're both out there.

Andre I don't really know and quite honestly, he kinda scares me a bit. I may not care as much what happens to him, but knowing he's out there with Dom gives me a little reprieve of my worry.

'Chloe!' Dom's voice travels through the cabin and I jump out of my skin. I race towards the door but stumble a little when I see he's alone. The look on his face says all I need to know.

Halting in my tracks, I fall to the ground and sobs rack my body. Oh God, my dad.

'Chloe, it's alright, I'm here, I've got you.' He pulls me up into his arms and I cling to him like he's my last breath.

'My dad? Dom please.'

'Chloe look at me. Chloe look at me baby.' His hand cradles my chin and he pulls my face to his. 'Your dad took on gunfire and was seriously injured by bullet to his stomach. Andre's taken him to one of his contacts, probably the same doctor who fixed me up. They're working on him now.'

'He's not dead?'

'No, honey, but it is touch and go. Andre will send us word when he can.'

'And Patrick? You got that fucker, right?' His deep inhale of breath tells me all I need to know before he even speaks.

'No, he wasn't there.' Anger mixed with sorrow shows in his eyes.

'What do we do now? Can we go to where my father is?' More tears roll down my cheeks and he uses the pad of his thumb to brush them away. 'I'd really like to be with him right now.'

'We can't, Chlo.' His mouth brushes mine, trying to soothe me. 'All we can do is wait for Andre to return with news.'

'And how long is that going to take?' I push away from him and throw myself down on the sofa.

'I don't know Chloe. I really don't know. I'm so sorry.' He comes and sits next to me, rubbing my back, trying to comfort me. Scooting me over, he lays beside me and pulls me into his arms, letting me cry out all the grief and worry. We must fall asleep, because as I open my eyes, I see that it's already light outside and panic takes hold. Andre hasn't shown up with any news.

'Dom, wake up, it's morning.' I shake his arm to get his attention and he grumbles something that sounds like 'No, no, I didn't kill him.' My heart races thinking of what that could imply. 'Dom, it's Chloe. Please get up. We haven't heard anything from Andre yet. What if my dad died while we slept the night away?'

'Chloe, calm down.' He mumbles as he pulls himself upright. 'I'm sure we would have heard from Andre if he'd died overnight. And, baby you needed to get some sleep.'

'You don't know that for sure, Dominic!'

'I'm sure we'll hear something soon. Let's just get a shower and clean-up to kill some time.'

'How could you possibly be thinking about sex right now at a time like this?'

He laughs. He fucking laughs.

'Chloe seriously, calm down.' Standing up, he pulls me into his arms, cradling me into his rock-hard body. I melt into him and I try my hardest not to respond, but my body betrays me. 'I wasn't thinking about sex, Chloe. But now that you mention it, would it really be so bad?' His nose caresses behind my ear as he trails it down my neck, suckling my sensitive nerves. My body trembles in response and he must be able to feel it.

'Dom…'

'Chlo, you said something to me before I left last night and I know this isn't the right time, but I need to show you how I feel.' My resolve crumbles as his lips crash into mine. I know it's all wrong in the moment, but I need this man. I need him inside me. I need to show him how much I love him. I need to feel his love. Something good needs to come from this whole shit-storm of a situation. *Amor vincit omnia*- Love conquers all, right?

Dom

CHLOE IS JUST about falling apart beneath me, her walls clenching, and the heels of her feet digging in to pull my ass closer. A knock on the door pauses my thrust mid push. I just need another minute to get us both off, but the second we hear it the moment disappears. Chloe starts scrambling out from beneath me.

'Oh god, Dom, I feel so bad now.' she whispers into my neck.

'Hey, people have sex in all kinds of fucked up situations, nothing wrong with what we just did.' I reassure her while pushing my delicate erection into my boxers.

'Aside from the fact that you have a massive bulge in your pants.' she motions to my cock as she throws her top on, there is no way of hiding it, or getting rid of it with someone hammering down the door, we're both still trying to get dressed when the knocking stops. Chloe almost kills herself pulling up her jeans and trying to take a step before her feet are all the way through, luckily she stops herself from face planting and scrambles to her feet and out through the bedroom door. A figure looms large outside the bedroom window and I jump. *Andre.* Fuck me. I motion for him to go back around front and then go to find Chloe who is stood at the open door, panic on her face.

'I think he left.'

'He didn't he's coming around now.' I rub her shoulder to reassure her. I don't know what the fuck he's here to tell us.

He's not even on the porch when she asks, 'Is he okay?'

Andre smiles and I sigh in relief. 'It'll take more than a stray bullet to take that stubborn fucker down.'

'Oh, thank god.' Her hands fly to her face and she starts to cry.

'Hey, I told you it would be okay didn't I?'

'I just kept thinking if that was the last time I'd see him. The last conversation we had, oh god, Dom, I wouldn't be able to live with myself.'

'I know but it's not, he's good, right?' I ask Andre.

Nodding he answers, 'He's good and has a pretty little nurse taking care of him.'

I bet he does. One that goes by the name Charity no doubt. 'Any chance I could grab a coffee before I go?'

'Of course,' Chloe answers and we all make our way to the kitchen. 'Was you with him all night?' I ask him.

'Yeah I stayed until the doc said he was out of the woods.'

'Thank you,' Chloe says and throws her arms around him. He looks a little surprised by it but soon relaxes and gives her a slight pat on her back. 'You must be exhausted let me make you something to eat?'

'No honestly I'm okay, just need some caffeine for the road, I'll grab some food and have a few hours sleep when I get home.' It's funny because for some reason it didn't even occur to me that he might actually live in the UK. Maybe he has a family? Wife and kids?

'Do you have kids?' Chloe asks like she read my mind.

'Nah I have a husband but no kids.'

Well fuck I never expected him to say he was gay, he's built like a fucking house and he'd scare most people with his dark looks and scary demeanour.

'Wow I didn't peg you at all.' Chloe giggles.

'Yeah most people are surprised.'

'I bet women hit on you all the time, right?' she asks. He smiles shaking his head but doesn't deny it.

'I better get going my better half has been blowing up my phone all morning worrying.'

'Does he know what you do for a living?'

'He does.' He doesn't elaborate anymore and honestly, I'm still reeling that he told us anything about himself at all.

'He must worry a lot?' Chloe adds.

Andre pops a brow and winces a little. 'Yeah unfortunately it's the worst part of being married to me, or so he says.'

'I can understand completely when you were all gone, that was the worst few hours of my life.' He smiles sympathetically, and I feel bad that she felt that way, so I pull her in for a hug.

Andre finishes up his coffee. 'I'm going to head out.' He lifts his cup. 'Thanks for that.'

'You're more than welcome.' Chloe tells him. We get to the front door,

'So as soon as Mike is well enough to move, I'll be bringing him to stay here, okay?'

'Umm yeah,' I answer because Chloe doesn't. Fucking great. Just what I need. Chloe is happy though, so I don't air my complaints.

My arms wrap around Chloe as we wave goodbye from the front step. My chin is on the warm skin of her shoulder. My dick comes back to life with unfinished business and I push up against her ass.

'Where were we?' I ask as she tilts her head up to kiss me.

'Mm, I think we were at a crucial point in the game.'

'Oh, I *know* we were.' I grab her up into my arms and carry her through to the bedroom, where I toss her onto the bed while she giggles as I pull off her jeans as she thrashes about trying to get them off. Fucking skinny jeans. She has no underwear on and I nuzzle between her thighs, which elicits a moan that goes straight to my dick. As I lick and suck my way to her orgasm I try to wriggle my way out of my joggers. It's harder than it looks and I fumble a little which makes her giggle.

'Fuck, I didn't want to stop.'

'How about trying this?' She flips me and straddles my face but that's not the best part, she does it reverse and reaches for my dick pushing my joggers down.

'Oh fuck yes!'

***
Chloe

It's been two days since Andre came with news of my dad. This morning when I made the coffee, my ears pricked up at a car coming down the gravel driveway. Grabbing Dom, I ran out to greet my father and Andre… But they weren't alone. Dom opened the car door and took my dad's arm wrapping it around his shoulder to take his weight and help him to the cabin. I went to close the door and a dainty little hand stopped me. Yep, Charity.

For the past 2 hours, and despite many attempts by Dom to get me to leave, I've been holed up in my room avoiding everybody in the house.

Why the fuck did he bring her here?

She could have just stayed wherever they were keeping her. I'm not going to lie, it's getting real difficult not to march up to her and punch her right in her pretty little face.

Maybe then some sense would be knocked into her.

'Chlo, I made some dinner for all of us. Will you please just come out and get some food?' Dom kisses me on the forehead, trying to soften the blow of what he's trying to make me do.

'I'm not sure I'll be able to keep the peace, Dom. Seriously, I look at her and my dad together and my blood just boils. It's all their fault we're in this situation and I'm just going to let them flaunt their twisted relationship in my face? I don't fucking think so.'

'Calm down, baby. Just come sit and eat. We all need to go over what needs to happen next and you haven't eaten all day. And besides, I'll be right next to you the whole time.' His tender lips meet mine and I know I'm going to do what he says. He's my saviour and I know he'd only do what's good for me.

'Fine.'

We all attempt to sit down at the little table in the corner of the kitchen, but we don't all fit. Andre opts to eat at the breakfast bar. Digging in, I try not to pay attention to anyone around me and just concentrate on my plate. That's until the conversation veers to Patrick.

'Have you got any word on where he could be now, Andre?' Dom questions.

'I heard earlier this evening he was hiding out in some warehouse in London. I was planning to check it out after I'm through here. I Just wanted to make sure everyone got settled first.'

'I'm coming.' Both Dom and my dad say at the same time.

'Really you don't have to. I'm just gonna do some recon and see if I can get a visual on the target.'

'No, I want to be there. We need to move as soon as we know he's there. We can't be losing this fucker again.'

'I'm in agreement. If it's only recon, then I'm well enough to tag along.' My dad chimes in.

'Alright we'll leave as soon as we're done here.'

'Sounds good.' Dom replies sounds anxious to get this whole ordeal over with.

Charity and my eyes connect across the table I think we both realise we won't get much choice in this matter. But there is one thing

I can control, and that's how I deal with her. I get up from the table and take the dishes into the kitchen. Charity grabs hers and my father's and follows me in.

Now is the perfect time.

'Can we speak for a moment?' Not really giving a choice, I extend my arm towards my room and she takes the hint.

Entering, I turn and close the door. No way I want them to hear.

'I know this isn't normal—'

I cut her off. 'I just have one question for you.' Her eyes plead, but I ignore it. 'Do you have some sort of mental impairment?'

'Um, no.' She looks confused, which affirms to me how young she really is.

'Do you think it's okay for you to be with a man in his fifties?'

'Well... well...'

'Let me try to put this in a way that you'd understand.' I pinch the bridge of my nose, I can feel a migraine coming on. 'You loved your father at one point, right? Probably still do even after all this.' She nods her head. 'How would you feel if he started having sex with one of your high school friends?'

'Eww, that's nasty. None of my friends would ever go for him though because he's always been so mean to them.' I can't help the loud huff of a laugh that pops out of my mouth. I'm now realizing that this is absolutely pointless. I thought it may be but was hoping it wasn't.

'Okay Charity, I see that I'm not really getting through to you. So, let's just drop it.' My hand reaches for the silver knob of the door when I realise she's not following behind me. The expression on her face surprises me when I turn to her.

'Listen, Chloe. I know you don't think much of me and I know it's hard for you to believe that Mike and I truly love each other, but we do.' My hand falls from the door knob and I turn to give her my full attention. 'I want to spend the rest of my life with him. Have you ever heard that saying that age is nothing but a number when it comes to love? Well that applies here. Even if me and him weren't thrown together under the circumstances we were, I still would have fallen for him. He's my soulmate and I'm his.' Her hand reaches out to rest on my shoulder, but she thinks twice and it falls halfway. 'You may think I don't understand where you're coming from, but I do. I just hope one day we can work past this.' Her face drops, unexpectedly my heart goes out to her. 'You scare me and make me nervous, Chloe, because I know that your dad respects you and one word from you and I'd be gone. He loves you that much, whether you know it or not. He's a great man and I'd do anything to remain in his life.' I'm left speechless as she turns and makes her way out of the room. Wow did that really just happen? I'll give her one thing, she sure has some lady balls on her. I can't deny that some of the things she said truly hit home.

CHAPTER TWENTY-ONE

Dom

AS WE LEAVE the house I look back at Chloe and Charity standing on the porch. The look on Chloe's face is a picture and for a second I wonder if it's sensible to leave them alone together. I look across at Mike—who was adamant he come along even though Andre said he wasn't leaving the van in his physical state—I find him also looking back at them both, no doubt worried we will come back to a cat fight. I decide to give him an out.

'Hey, Mike you sure you're feeling up to doing this?'

'What the fuck does that mean? I've told you already I'm going.'

I lower my voice 'I'm just not sure it's wise leaving them together.' I throw him a look telling him what I mean. He gets it. And then he slows his pace.

'You know what Andre I think it's probably best if I stay behind.' He calls out to Andre who's leading the way.

'I couldn't agree more, you need the rest.' Andre nods.

'Somehow I don't see me getting any rest with those two.' He indicates their way discreetly. Andre chuckles and we wait while he heads back and I wave at Chloe while Charity throws her arms around Mike. I shudder at what Chloe must be thinking right now. As we get into Andre's van he laughs out loud as he starts the van.

'Glad I'm not the one dealing with that shit show,' he says as we pull out of the drive.

'I thought Chloe was going to lose her shit at dinner, the atmosphere was fucking awful,' I agree.

'I know! Why'd you think I ate at the breakfast bar.' He grins. 'I'm sure it will all work out for the best.'

'Does Charity even know what we're doing here?' I ask.

'She knows.' He nods as we pull out of the small winding road.

'And she's okay with that? You know us killing her dad?' I reiterate.

'Look, all I know is he's a bad motherfucker who tried to sell her like a possession.'

'I guess, yeah… I can see why she'd be okay with it when you put it like that. So how sure are you that he's there?'

'I'm positive he was there earlier, whether he's still there now? Not so sure, but I have eyes on the place and somewhere like that isn't easy to get out of without being seen. I'm hoping we can put this shit to bed tonight.'

'Here's hoping.'

'You okay with it?'

'Killing Patrick?' He nods. 'Fuck no, I'm not, but I know it's the only way so I've made my peace with it. I don't know if this is your usual line of work but I'd be lying if I said the mere thought of ending another life doesn't make me feel sick.'

'It gets easier,' he reassures me. But it doesn't make me feel better about what I did or what we're about to do. Its fucking hard, I see that man take his last breath every time I close my eyes. It's not fun, and I truly hope that it does get easier. I try to change the subject.

'How's your husband?'

He side glances at me. 'He's fine.'

'What's his name?'

'Greg.' He looks at me again like he's mildly amused at my line of questioning.

'Cool, you been married long?'

'Two years'

'Who asked who?'

'Are you nervous?'

'Just trying to lighten the mood and make things easier, you don't have to answer if you don't want to.'

'I asked him, in Paris on the Passerelle des Arts bridge we'd just put our padlock on there and as he threw the key into the river I got down on one knee.'

I smile. 'That's real romantic, I wouldn't have guessed you'd be the romantic type.'

'Yeah I'm not just a bodyguard and personal hit man.'

'Definitely more than a pretty face, huh.' We both laugh. As we near the spot he'd chosen for us to watch from he gets quiet and I'm glad because as we pull to a stop I swallow and try to get in my own headspace. Mentally prepare for what I hope ends tonight.

***

Chloe

I stand in the doorway and watch the love of my life pull away down the drive. Not knowing what will happen is killing me. Him being with Andre makes me feel a little better, but hell, look what happened to my dad. Some things are just avoidable.

My heart sits painfully in my stomach. I turn as they disappear from sight and come face to face with Charity in my father's arms. Quickly walking past, them, I try to make my way through the doorway only to be stopped by Dad's hand on my shoulder.

'Please don't run, Chloe.' His eyes plead with mine.

'I just can't right now, Dad. I'm sorry.' My tears begin to fall as soon as the bedroom door closes behind me. Never in a million years did I ever expect to be in this type of situation. Never in a million years did I expect to fall in love with a stranger. Yes, we' aren't strangers anymore, but I'd be lying to myself if I said I hadn't loved him from the beginning. My Colton in shining armour. My saviour. My love.

Wiping the tears from my cheeks, I suck it up and start gathering my clothes to shower and get ready for bed. Granted, I don't think I'll be getting much sleep, but I have to try in case Dom needs me when he returns. I pull some pyjama pants out of the drawer and am reaching for a tee when I spot Dom's shirt laying on the dresser in a crumpled-up mess. I grab it and head across the hall to the bathroom.

'Chloe wait. Can we please talk, honey?' My dad catches me just as I get one foot into the bathroom.

'I'm about to shower, can it wait?'

'Can you meet me in the living room when you're done?' Wetness pools in his eyes and the softie inside of me relents.

'Yes.'

'Okay. Good. Great. I'll see you in a little bit. I can see if I can find some hot cocoa in the cupboards. It can be like old times.' Old times... Pish posh, not in this lifetime, but I will hear him out, again.

My shower is longer than I expected. The house is quiet and it's starting to get dark outside by the time I emerge. The hairs on the back on my neck stick up and my ears go on alert. I know my dad wouldn't go to bed before talking to me. Not with the look he'd on his face before walking away. I take the steps down slowly, trying to be as quiet as I can. I could be overreacting, but the feeling in my stomach tells me different. When I get to the hallway, I turn cautiously to the right, towards the kitchen. Just as I'm turning, a dirty, stinky hand comes across my mouth and pulls my hands behind me. From that smell alone, I know exactly who it is.

'I'm going to take my hand off of your mouth. Don't try screaming or you'll regret it.' He moves his hand from my mouth but keeps a tight grip on my arms.

'We're in the middle of nowhere. Who do you expect to hear me scream? And after all these times you've already kidnapped me, have I screamed even once?'

'Just shut up. All this hiding and running I've been doing isn't allowing me to think clearly. And you know how I get when I can't think clearly.' Patrick runs the tips of his fingers down my cheek and then caresses my neck. I don't know what the fuck is going on, but I sure as hell don't like the direction it's going. All my time spent with him and he's never attempted to get this close. He really must be scattered. All the sudden I hear someone struggling in the corner of the kitchen I try and glance over, only to see Dad on the floor.

'Dad.' I yell over to him and Patrick clamps his hand back over my mouth.

'Now now, little missy, I thought I said no yelling.' That's when it hits me. He really is a vile man. He's going to molest me in front of my father as some form of payback. Is he going to rape me? I struggle against his grip and my knees give out under me. He releases my mouth and both hands grab me under the arms.

'Where's Charity? Did you take her?'

'Don't worry where the fuck *my daughter* is. At this point, *sweetheart*, I think you need to worry about yourself.' His foul whisky breath hits my nostrils as he bellows in my face.

'Get off me!' I yell back at him. A loud bang echoes and I see my dad hit his head on the bottom cabinet in the kitchen. His eyes close as if he's knocked himself out from struggling so hard. 'Come on, Patrick, you know you've never gone this far before. My dad is unconscious, there's no one to get back at right now. You have Charity. Please just stop.'

'Oh no, sweet pea. I've already started. And believe me, I always finish the things I start.' He tosses me up against the breakfast bar and pushes my head down towards the surface. My pyjama pants are yanked down and he grinds his hard-on against my ass. Bile rises in my throat and I turn my head to try to bring in air. Oh my God is this really going to happen? After all this time, I thought this was all coming to an end. When I hear his zipper going down, I try and struggle back against him, but immediately halt as I realize it's turning him on more.

Please Dad, come to. I need you right now more than I ever have!

CHAPTER TWENTY-TWO

Dom

WE SIT IN the van for well over an hour before we see any kind of movement. Cars start leaving in a procession. But we don't see Patrick in any of them. Andre is still confident he's inside so we sit tight. He sends some men after the procession just in case. I have a bad feeling about all this, which I'm sure is just nerves. But something just doesn't feel right. I don't know how to explain this feeling to Andre so I don't say shit, he's the expert. I'm here just because of circumstance. But I'll be damned if Patrick's going to hurt anyone I love again.

I close my eyes against the thought of losing Chloe or my nan, and who I've already lost because of that bastard. Nah that's not happening again while I can draw breath. I've made my peace with killing him, Chloe not so much but she knows it has to happen. And if it means choosing between living without looking over our shoulders, or a life on the run, fearing everyday might be our last, there isn't a choice. Even if Chloe doesn't want me after what I have to do, she'll be safe. My nan will be safe. That's my priority and the driving force fuelling my mind-set.

He has to die.

And, I'm prepared to do that at a moment's notice.

Andre glances at me as the last car leaves and then with his binoculars he checks the passengers. He shakes his head. Patrick motherfucking Smith is still inside. We make our way up toward the entrance we've been watching. Andre radios his men and has them in position in minutes. We haven't heard anything from the others who followed the procession. No news is good news, right? We go into the building pretty much like we did the house the last time. We creep through the floor space which looks like it has been set up as a casino. The place is deserted though as if everyone just upped and left in an emergency. Money and chips still line the tables. I look around and that uneasy feeling comes back with a vengeance. I glance to Andre who looks just as worried as I feel.

'Fuck,' he says, as his men come into sight at the other side of the enormous room. 'We need to move he could be anywhere.'

'But why leave all this?' I motion around.

'Because he fucking knew we were here.'

'Fucking hell' I growl pissed off at our stupidity. 'We need to find them, have your guys still got eyes on them?'

Andre grabs his radio, his usual cool slipping 'Have you still got eyes?' he shouts. The radio crackles and my heart hammers in my chest as we wait on an answer.

'Affirmative'

Andre nods his head to me 'Time to move.' His guys are on their tail giving us their coordinates, we jump in the van and follow at speed, we have a lot of distance to make up.

'Do not fucking lose them,' is the last thing Andre growls into his radio. He floors the accelerator and we drive through country lanes like boy racers. I check my seatbelt twice bracing myself for an impact at any second as all four wheels come off the road at a dip, but Andre keeps the van under control and we speed around corners that shouldn't be taken at more than thirty miles per hour. I send up a little prayer that we don't die before we catch that motherfucker. But Andre is skilled at driving at speed and before we know it, the procession of cars is in the distance. We don't get too close so he can't make us out. But we stay within a safe distance and follow until they turn off onto what looks like a farmland road.

Andre turns off the headlights as we pass our guys on the side road getting out of their vehicles and moving forward on foot. Parking up in front we wait for them to catch up. As two of them stand at Andre's window they pass on their feedback. They tell us one vehicle turned off about ten miles back. Andre's man Cody is in pursuit. Andre nods thinking about that for a minute.

'Do you think it's likely to be him?' I ask impatiently.

'What's their direction?' The guy shrugs a little perplexed.

Andre gets on his radio. 'Cody where are you?'

'Boss it looks like we could be heading to somewhere near the safe house.'

'How close?' he asks urgently.

My fucking heart is in my mouth and I can't speak. The fear of Patrick being where Chloe is, after everything, is beyond comprehensible right now. I start to run back to the van. Andre is torn I can tell, it could be a trap to lead us away, but they could fucking know where the safe house is. I rev the van up and look to Andre giving him a last chance to jump in. He doesn't and I spray the road with dirt as I try to turn the vehicle around in the small ass space. As I pass him he waves me to a stop and comes to the driver's door.

'I'll drive, get out.' I don't argue and climb across the gear stick and strap in.

As we take off down the road and make our way to the safe house, Andre calls on the radio. 'Cody come in... Cody?' He's met with silence. 'Cody check in? CODY!' 'Fuuuuuck' he hits the steering wheel. I didn't honestly think we could go any faster but surprisingly we do, and I'm not complaining. As we pull down the drive nothing seems out of place, but we turn off the headlights and drive as quietly as possible toward the house. I'm jumping out of the van before we've even pulled to a stop. I hear Andre call me back but I'm not in the right frame of mind to listen to orders. I just want to see Chloe safe. I'm desperate as I fling open the front door.

'CHLOE?'

***

Chloe

'How do we get back in to get Mike?' Charity cries as we hunch behind the shed in the back of the cabin. After Patrick had yanked my pyjama bottoms off, my struggling ceased and I thought maybe that that would get him to stop. No man wants no response from a woman, no matter the situation. But no, next thing I knew, his fingers found their way into my panties and he tried to work my clit into submission, but my lady parts weren't up for playing. Me being bone dry pissed him off even more because he couldn't the reaction or satisfaction that he thought he would. With one more hard thrust of his disgusting finger inside me, he released me and went over to my father, looking as if he was trying to rouse him. I jumped out of my skin as Charity grabbed my arm and whispered, 'Let's go'. We snuck around the corner just as Patrick kicked my dad in the ribs. I had to hold Charity back from running to him. Dragging her out the back door as quietly as I could, we made our way back here behind the shed, not wanting to go too far so that we could go back for my dad.

'I don't know Charity.' Just as the words leave my mouth, Patrick starts screaming in the cabin. 'Let's wait to see if he heads out here after us and then we can try to sneak back in and get my dad out of there.' I reach over and pull her toward me, hugging her to my side. I know both us women have been through a lot and whether I like her it not, she did just save my life. I owe her one.

'I think I can handle that. Do you want to split up or go in together?'

'I think we should stick together. I don't want to risk him getting a hold of one of us again and if we're together, that'd be two of us to fight back at once.'

Lights flash as though someone just pulled down the drive, quickly followed by more flashes of headlights beaming off the tree to the east side of the cabin. My heart begins to race harder than it already was, he's brought reinforcements. There's no way I'm telling Charity what that means for us. Him alone we could handle. Him with his goons, not so much. We're going to have to leave my dad behind for now.

'Chloe!' My name bellows through the forest. It's Dom. Oh my god, it's Dom.

'Is that Dominic?' Charity asks as she starts to get up and move towards the direction of his voice, only for me to pull her back down to squatting position.

'Charity, Get down. We can't give away where we are yet.' I slowly bring my head around the corner of the shed to see if there's anyone outside the back of the cabin. It looks like it's all clear. 'Okay, we're going to slowly make our way around the side of the cabin and try to get out towards the woods. Dom has to have the van somewhere. We'll try to get to it and radio Andre from there. He keeps a CV attached to the dash. Understand?'

'What about Mike?'

'If Dom is here, so is Andre. Andre will get him out. His loyalties are to my dad. Let's go.' I grab her hand and we make our way around the shed, trying our best to keep to the shadows. Nearing the house, I hear men talking but pay them no mind as I focus on which direction we need to head into the woods. That's until I hear Dom's voice echo off of the walls inside the cabin.

'Where is she damnit? So help me, I'll break every goddamned bone in your body if you don't tell me where she is.' The sound of the crunch of bones hits my ears and I can't help but cringe.

'I told you, they escaped. Both of them, the fucking filthy tramps.' There's more sounds of fists hitting bone and I know we need to get to the van ASAP. Dom needs to know that I'm okay, that we're both okay.

'Come on.' This time it's Charity pulling me along as we start to wade our way through the heavy brush of the woods. It's pitch dark and we both stumble a time or two before I spot the van Andre and Dom left in earlier this evening.

'That's the van.' We both break out in a sprint towards it, Charity losing her footing one more time before reaching the sliding back door. I throw it open and we both dive in. 'Are you alright, Charity?'

'No, I think my ankle's broke. But don't worry about me right now. Get the men. Save Mike please.' Tears stream down her face and I'm sure the pain of the break is overwhelming her as well as fear of losing the love of her life. I move my way to the front of the van and grab the CV receiver off of the holder.

'Andre, come in. Andre, it's Chloe.' My voice squeaks as I try to get the words out.

'Chloe, where are you?' He replies within seconds.

'I'm in the van. Charity is with me, but Dom and my dad are still in the house with Patrick.'

'Stay put, don't go anywhere.'

CHAPTER TWENTY-THREE

Dom

I'M SO DONE with this fucker, I'm going to beat him to death if he doesn't tell me where Chloe is. His face is a mess and I'm having trouble seeing him my vision is so blurred. Arms wrap around me and yank me off and I swing for that motherfucker too.

'Dom it's me.' Andre's words filter through the red mist and I huff out a tired breath, I feel like I just fought ten rounds. I stumble back and Andre takes in the scene.

'The girls are in the van.' I look at him with disbelief. Is it really that easy? We have her back? 'Go,' he tells me stepping over Patrick, going to Mike's aid. I leave the cabin and look for the van with my gun drawn in case I come across anyone else. It feels like forever before I get the van door open.

I take in the sight before me and almost fall to my knees. Chloe scrambles on her hands and knees toward me and climbs into my arms.

'Oh thank god you're alive.' She sobs in my ear. Clutching me so tight around my neck I'm almost choking.

I chuckle. 'Babe you need to let me breathe.' She lets go she clasps my face in between her hands.

'Is Mike okay?' Charity calls from further inside the van, also in tears. They're both filthy and look like they've been dragged through a hedge. I can't answer her though because I didn't pay much attention to Mike.

'Come on we'll go find out.' I take her hand —she's shaking so hard her teeth are chattering— and we climb out. I spot she's wearing only a t-shirt that barely covers her ass. Her eyes meet mine as I'm about to ask why she's half naked.

'I was in the shower when he came.' Her eyes flit to Charity and back to me. 'It was all I could grab,' she explains.

As I open the door to the kitchen the first thing I notice is the pool of blood by Patricks mouth. He's still out cold and Mike is now up on his feet untied and being tended to by Andre. Charity runs past the both of us and throws her arms around him. I take my jacket off and hand it to Chloe, and she wraps it around her waist.

I stare intently at Mike. 'Was he alone? Have you seen anyone else?'

He looks up and shakes his head. 'I didn't see anyone else he completely blindsided me.' His hand reaches up to the huge bleeding lump on his head. Chloe dashes off to the bathroom and as I go to follow her I notice her PJ pants on the floor by the counter. I close my eyes against the pain tightening my chest. That red mist lowers once more and as it descends I hear a groan at my feet.

'You bastard' I kick Patrick in the ribs once twice and again in the head, but it doesn't satisfy me. As I pull my foot back aiming it at his skull Charity cries out behind me.

'Stop please.'

'He needs to fucking die.' I growl at her.

'Go.' Andre lifts his chin telling me to go after Chloe. 'I'll secure him. I turn without another word and go after her. I find her scrubbing herself in the shower. I strip and go in behind her reaching for the loofah she's using. As my hand touches hers she screams and jumps forward away from me.

'It's me, baby it's just me.' I reassure her.

Collapsing into my arms she cries silently, as her body shakes in my arms, all I can do is hold her. I want to know what he did to her, I need to know what he did, but at this moment in time I can't ask her. This is what she needs from me. Just this and nothing more.

As I hold her, the images I have in my mind of her half naked and finding her pj bottoms on the floor in the kitchen work me over like some evil invader. I can't get the horrible pictures out of my mind. A cry rips out from inside me, and I'm just as shocked as Chloe as she looks up into my eyes, the water cascading down her back.

'Did he… Did he…' I swallow the lump in my throat as I try desperately to get the words out. 'I'm so sorry Chloe, I'm so fucking sorry.' I squeeze her tight to my chest.

'He didn't rape me,' she says so quietly I can barely hear her over the din of the water. Relief floods through me, but then she hiccups. 'He tried. But, Charity got me out.'

'Thank god for Charity,' I say barely able to keep my emotions in check. 'You need to talk about it?' I offer but she shakes her head she isn't ready, and honestly neither am I. I hold her tight and let her cry into my chest.

***

Chloe

Dom carries me from the bathroom straight into our room and gently lays me down on the bed.

He covers me and then tosses on his sleep shorts and t-shirt. I try to will the tears to stop falling from my eyes, but I just can't. They're tears of pain, and anguish and tears of happiness for this finally being over. Dom pulls me even closer and the wetness from his own tears hit my skin.

'Baby I'm alright. We're alright now.' Dom says. I pull away enough to bring his face closer.

Clasping his strong jaw in my hand, I bring his mouth to mine, tenderly kissing the pain away. My lips move to his cheeks and kiss away his tears too. His hands thread through my hair and he brings my lips back to his.

'I'm so sorry I let that bastard get to you, baby.' He gently sucks my bottom lip into his mouth. 'I'm so fucking sorry.' He puts all his feelings into kissing me and I take in all that I can.

'I love you, Dominic.'

'I love you too.' I look deep into his multi-coloured eyes and I see the truth that they hold. This man has been through everything for me. Put himself and the people he holds dear in danger. All to save me. I pull him in and put everything I have into kissing him, showing him how much I love him in return.

The feeling the need to wash away everything that's happened and replace it with love and happiness, I reach down, grabbing the hem of his grey cotton shirt and pull it over his head.

'We don't have to do this, Chloe.'

'I need you, Dom. I need you.' His lips meet mine once again, but this time with vigour and a purpose. His hands caress my sides as they make their way to the place where I need him the most. He nibbles down my neck reaching his lips for my nipple. As he pulls it into his mouth he inserts a finger into my soaking wet pussy. I moan out at the sensations and my body lifts towards him.

'I need you inside me, Dom, *now.*' My gaze pleads with his. 'Please, Dom.' The emptiness from him removing his finger is filled only seconds later as I feel him there, rubbing my wetness back and forth, preparing to enter me. In one swift movement, he's there my body begins to tremble. 'Make love to me, Dominic.' And he does. Slowly bringing me to the edge and then letting me come back down before doing it all over again. His mouths meets mine one last time before his strokes start to become frantic as he tightens within me. My hips raise up to meet his, both of us releasing at the same time.

Collapsing down on top of me, we remain there until our breathing evens and my heart rate makes it back to normal. He raises his eyes and meets mine.

'Chloe, when this is all over with, will you marry me? Right away. No waiting.' My heart stops. The look on his face tells me he's for real. But seriously, who am I kidding.

'Yes. Yes, I will.' My heart soars as he pulls me into his arms, placing small kisses all over my forehead.

In that moment, a scary thought crosses my mind. Oh my God, the other guys that drove up.

'Dom, there were a least two more vehicles that drove up when Charity and I were hiding out behind the shed. Did you guys find them?'

'What? No, we didn't find anyone else. Shit.' He jumps out of bed and throws on some basketball shorts. The door practically slams open and then closed behind him, leaving me with only the sound of his pounding footsteps as he runs down the hall.

Chapter Twenty-Four

Dom

'ANDRE?' I SHOUT as I near the kitchen, 'Andre?'

'I'm here? What is it?' He comes through the door into the hall.

'Chloe said there were others, Patrick wasn't alone. Did your men sweep the grounds?' The look on his face tells me they didn't. How could we be so fucking stupid. 'Get them back here now, we need to make sure this place is secure.'

He gets on the phone 'Where are you?' he asks right away, 'turn around we need the grounds sweeping.' He covers the speaker and looks to me. 'I'm so fucking tired I need to get my head in the game.' He's obviously annoyed with himself.

'They far away?' I ask a little on edge.

'Not far away thankfully.' He starts making plans and as he does that I head back to the bedroom, I'm not leaving Chloe alone when Patrick's men could be anywhere.

'Is everything okay?' she asks, worry all over her face.

I nod. 'Yeah, babe but you need to get dressed okay? I want you to stay with your dad and Charity while we check out the woods. You need to all be together.'

'Of course.' She pulls on some joggers and one of my t-shirts which buries her but the sight of her in my clothes is still a turn on even in this fucked up situation. She catches me looking at her and gives me a small smile as she takes my hand. 'I'm ready,' she says although there's a tremor in her tone.

We find the others in the kitchen and I watch as Chloe's eyes linger on the discarded PJ bottoms on the floor. I move her past them and pick them up throwing them into the rubbish bin. She doesn't say anything about it but she doesn't object. I look to Andre for an ETA on his men.

'They're only about fifteen minutes out. They've just turned around and come back.'

'It was stupid to assume he was alone,' Mike chastises.

'Mike, we never saw anyone leave the warehouse beforehand, it was a bad call, I'm sorry.'

'Sorry won't cut it when we get attacked because you took your eye off the ball.' He sounds like he has a mouth full of cotton wool when he speaks because his face is such a mess.

'We won't. I've been vigilant.'

Mike makes a sound like he's scoffing at his answer but it comes out kind of strangled.

'Boss you need to rest, you should sit down and relax a bit' Andre motions toward the lounge.

Charity hasn't stopped fucking about with a sponge and water dabbing at his face.

He wafts her away with his hand. 'No, I'd rather stay in here.' He turns to Charity. 'Stop fucking fussing I'm fine.' He tries to wave her off him again but she's relentless and I almost laugh but hold it in. Only Chloe hears the snort I make in the back of my throat, it makes her smile and bite her lip as she also tries not to laugh. I take a gun from the counter and check the chamber making sure I'm good to go if needed and sit at the opposite side of the table to Mike and Charity. I indicate for Chloe to sit on my lap, and she comes willingly, resting her head in the crook of my neck and shoulder. This. This is what I want to be able to do on the daily without any threats. And she said yes. Fuck, we're going to get hitched!

'Do you mind if I speak with my dad?' Charity asks of no one in particular just throwing it out in the room. We all look at each other and I'm not really sure I should answer, so I say nothing. But then neither does anyone else.

'Charity do you really think that's wise? Given the circumstance?' Chloe asks. I feel a prickle of pride at my girl.

'He's still my dad, and he won't hurt me.'

'Oh sure, he was just going to sell you off to a fucking evil bastard for money.' Mike chimes in. But it doesn't hold any weight with her because she ignores it completely.

'He won't physically harm me,' she says looking at Chloe.

'Don't look at me for an answer. You're clearly going to do what you want regardless.' Chloe snaps back.

'I know it's hard for you all to understand but—'

'But you still love him, even after everything he's put you through put us through?' Chloe snaps again. Charity nods but has the decency to look ashamed about it.

'He was going to *rape* me!' She raises her voice now. 'And what? You want to go down there and tell him you still love him?' Charity suddenly finds her feet very interesting. But she says nothing. 'Just go, you're going to anyway.' Chloe spits the words like venom.

Mike shakes his head at Charity trying to get her to reconsider, but she walks to the door and heads out of sight to the basement. Chloe glares at Mike and I'm not sure what she was about to say but Charity shouts up the stairs.

'He's gone!'

I haul ass past Charity and find his bindings cut through and a window smashed in the corner. Andre is only a second behind me and he's cursing the air blue. Mike hobbles to the top of the stairs with Chloe at his back and we all look down in disbelief. Why is shit never easy? As we all get back to the kitchen we hear two vans pull up. Andre moves the net curtain and peeks out, he visibly relaxes and opens the door letting his men inside.

'Dom and I will stay inside with everyone, I want you all to fan out and find that greasy bastard.' I look over to Chloe who looks pale and like she just might be sick. I grab some water and wet a kitchen towel, kneeling in front of her.

'Chlo, you okay?'

'Mm.' She nods but it's bullshit. 'I'm...' she swallows and looks like she's going to be sick. 'I'm just going...' snapping her mouth closed she dashes for the bathroom and I follow to make sure she's okay. She's obviously scared out of her mind now that he's on the loose again. Fuck we should have taken extra precautions. I'm about to close the door behind us and hold back her hair when a gunshot sounds from somewhere close.

***

Chloe

My head is deep in the toilet heaving up everything I've had to eat and drink today as I hear a gunshot go off behind me. It echoes in the toilet bowl while my head is in it and my ears ring.

'Stay here.' Dom commands, with instructions to lock the door after he closes it. I can't hear any talking outside the bathroom, only a lot of shuffling around, right before I hear another two gunshots. A knock sounds at the door.

'Chloe, it's me. Let us in quickly.' Dad's voice filters through the wood of the door and I rush over flip the lock off. Him and Charity rush in the bathroom and he pushes her into the bathtub and whispers for her to stay down before turning to me and trying to give me the same command.

'No dad, I don't need to be in the tub. You climb in with her and take cover.' Even with all the adrenaline running through me, I turn towards the toilet once again and dry heave into it.

'Chloe, this is the second time since I've been here that you've thrown up. Is it really just the stress and everything or is there something else going on?' He questions as he lifts his leg and climbs into the tub next to Charity. She climbs onto his lap once he's down. The sight of that alone makes me want to hurl again.

'What do you mean?' I ask as I grab a hair tie off of the countertop and tie my hair back.

'Could you be...' He motions his hands around Charity's stomach, indicating a pregnant belly. 'You know. Pregnant?'

'What? Wait. No, I am *not* pregnant. At what point in all the months that I've been fighting *your* battles do you think that I've had time to go and get myself knocked up.' Truth is, I really don't know. And now I think about it, I haven't had my period since before the first time I was held captive. But wait didn't we use protection? Fuck, I can't even remember. Shit could I be? Wait, why the fuck are we even having this conversation right now when the love of my life is out there in danger?

'No, Chloe that's not fair on Charity and me. Her father is to blame for all of this. I was just doing the right thing.' His defences go up.

'I don't know, dad, but I'll tell you what I do know.' My anger is starting to boil. 'Charity was down in the basement for a few moments before she called up and told us that he was gone.' I point an accusatory finger in her direction. 'You could have easily untied him and boosted him up and out that window down there.' I look to Charity. 'We all know how much you love your *daddy*.'

'Chloe Marie Richards how dare you speak to her that way. You know damn well she didn't help him escape. You're not only insulting her right now but you're insulting me. I won't stand for that young lady.'

'*Young lady*? Are you seriously calling me young lady while you have a nineteen year old little *girl* straddled on your lap? One that I'm pretty certain you've already stuck it to.'

'Hey.' Charity whisper yells but my dad cuts her off quickly.

'Chloe I'm going to give you a pass right now because of the situation we're currently in but when this is all done, all three of us are sitting down for a little chat.

'Four,' I correct him in a whisper.

'This is not the time, no matter how upset you are. Fine four. I didn't know if you expected to keep Dom around when all this is over,' he whispers back.

'I need something to focus on or I'm about to lose my shit…' I'm cut off by footsteps running down the hall and a hushed whisper outside the door.

'Chloe? Chloe, open up.' It's Dom's voice and I crack the door open enough to let him in. 'I just wanted to update you before Andre and I head off to take Pete to Andre's doctor, he's been hit.'

'What's going on?'

'He got away but we managed to take down a few of his comrades before they all retreated. Right now, we need to get Pete to the docs. Here take this.' He hands me a gun and another to my dad. 'You make sure you stay together and Mike anything happens to her, I'll kill you myself.' He looks at my dad with searing intensity in his eyes. 'I'll be back as soon as possible.' He pulls my face to his and kisses me long and hard. 'I love you,' he whispers against my lips and then closes the door gently behind him. His footsteps retreat down the hall and when they've finally ceased, I turn and slump against the bathroom door and I slide down as it hits me even harder that Patrick is still alive and he's still out there threatening our lives. Oh and then there's the fact that there could be a baby growing in my belly and I didn't even have time to tell the man I love.

CHAPTER TWENTY-FIVE

Dom

I WAS RELUCTANT to go with Andre, leaving Chloe behind didn't sit well with me but someone has to drive while Andre puts pressure on the wound. And I know where the doc's is because I've been before. I was hoping I'd never have to go back but here we are. I'm driving at full speed down the country roads and I honestly don't know how we haven't skidded off into the ditch but my adrenaline must have my reactions on point. About four miles down the road I spot a four by four just like the ones Patricks men were driving as they left the warehouse. As we get closer a shot fires and I swerve not knowing which direction it came from. The windscreen cracks as another shot rings out. Shit.

'What the fuck is going on?' Andre shouts from the back.

'Fuckers are shooting at us, hold on.' I slam my foot down on the clutch and go up a gear, picking up speed I ram the back of the car, making it swerve, but it rights itself quickly. Fuck. I accelerate and try to overtake, at least that way I can shoot too. But they swerve all over the road not letting me pass. A gun comes out of the side window and I'm pretty certain I'm done. Slamming the brakes, I swerve and hit the back of the car, it flips in the air, and we spin out of control, Andre and Pete flying around like pinballs in the back.

Thank fuck I have my seatbelt on because otherwise I'd be through the windshield. I have my gun in my hand and the steering wheel in the other. I'm desperately trying to right the spin. There is so much noise the crunching of metal and screeching of tires, leaving a ringing noise in my ears. When we finally stop spinning I'm so fucking disoriented with my head spinning, I leap out of the van and run in the wrong direction for a few seconds. A loud blast has me flying through the air. My ears are scream an unbearable keening that rips the atmosphere apart. My head snaps back on my neck as I hit the ground.

'Urgh.' I roll around for a second trying to get my bearings. I find the source of the explosion and quickly realise it's the car we were chasing. It feels like it's miles away as I start to make my way toward it. I hold my gun up on shaky hands as I see someone in the ditch, crawling away. Patrick. Just seeing him centres me. I should be checking on Andre and Pete. But this can end here. With one bullet, I can finish it.

'Patrick,' I growl. He continues crawling through the grass away from me. That red mist descends as I think about what he did to Chloe. And I don't hesitate. I stand over him and pull him up and around so he's facing me. But I can't squeeze the trigger. I push the barrel of the gun to his forehead.

His eyes widen but then he grins. 'You better kill me, motherfucker, because I won't stop, and next time I'll rape that pretty little pussy—' I squeeze the trigger cutting him off mid-sentence. I fire two more into his chest to make sure. I make sure no one is alive in the wreck of the car before I move to the van to check on Andre.

I open the side door and find Andre unconscious. I'm too late for Pete. An explosion like that will have caused someone call the emergency services. I battle with whether I should leave Pete behind but I decide that should be Andre and Mike's call, so I pull the door closed get into the driver's seat and make my way back to the house. Groaning in the back has me craning my neck to check on Andre, but I don't slow down. Sirens wail in the distance and I put my foot down, gunning it all the way down the winding track and pulling up with screeching brakes around the back.

'What happened?' Andre blinks in confusion. He looks down at Pete. My ears are still ringing and I have a headache from hell. But as I help him out the van he demands answers.

'We ran into Patrick and we spun out of control. There was an explosion. I shot Patrick he's dead.'

'Pete's gone,' he tells me like it's not blindingly obvious.

'I'm sorry,' I offer, but he doesn't say anything else until we get to the back door.

'You sure he's dead?'

'Fucking positive.'

'Good, keep it between us for now.' He seems to have realised something and turns to look back at the van.

'Damage.' He points to the driver's side 'We need to get rid of it quickly.' He doesn't even hesitate he hops right into it.

'Go on in and tell Mike we hit a problem and I'll be back as soon as I can.'

'Andre you're a mess man?'

'No time for that now, we need this gone, if the police come looking we can't have it sitting on the drive.' I cringe at the mere thought of that, and I know he's right.

'Okay but keep your phone on okay?'

'Roger that.' I watch as he turns the van around and pulls back down the winding path. I smell like fire and I feel like I've been in a fight with a truck. That explosion blew me off my feet and I hit my head pretty fucking hard. I look down at myself. I'm a fucking mess and I'm covered in blood. Patrick's blood.

***

Chloe

Even though I wanted Dom to be there for the talk with my father, Charity and I had, it couldn't be avoided seeing as we were all stuck in the same house and my father wasn't about to let it go. The bathroom started to get stifling with us all crammed in, so we moved in a hunched together group over to the room Dom and I have been sharing since we've been at the cabin. I let everything out to them about how I felt about their relationship. From the fact that she's not even old enough to drink yet where we're from, to her being the reason we're all in this situation. Zoe was killed as a result of it all. I had to bite my lip to keep from tearing up over Zoe. Charity had tears flowing down her face the entire time. At least it's good to know she's resentful.

Then my dad proceeded to tell me how Patrick was planning on trading off Charity in a business deal and he grabbed her to keep her from the family she was going to. When he heard the plans and the name of the family she was getting traded to, he knew he had to help her. The McCanns are ruthless heathens. He's seen first-hand how they treat their women and there was no way he could let that happen to an innocent girl. It didn't help that the first time he ever laid eyes on her, he claimed he fell in love. Love at first sight is what he called it. She was always in the background when he'd been at the gambling halls ran by Pat.

Charity barely spoke other than to reiterate to me that she truly did love my father and planned on spending the rest of her life with him. Gag. She wants to have a relationship with me, but at this point in time, I'd be happy to just go back to not having my dad in my life, just as it was prior to this whole ordeal.

I hear a door creaking open somewhere in the house and we all go on alert. I wave Charity and my dad back into the corner of the room and put my finger to my lips signalling them to be quiet. My dad struggles against Charity to get over to me, but she holds him back. With one hand braced against the back of the door, I turn the knob and as quietly as possible, open it enough to peek through. The moment the door opens, the smell of burning hits my nostrils. With my one eye peeking through, I watch. There's a tall man slowly making his way towards the bathroom across the hall. He pushes the door open and disappears inside only to pop his head back through it a moment later.

'Dom?' My voice booms through the hall louder than expected and he quickly turns in my direction, gun pulled.

'Chloe?'

'Yes, we're over here.' He lowers the gun and tucks it into his waistband. When he comes into full view I finally take him in. From head to toe. He's covered in blood and he's where the smell of smoke is coming from. 'Dom, what happened? Are you hurt?' I rush to him and look him over but he holds me back at arm's length.

'It's not my blood, baby. I'm okay. I really need a shower though.' He grasps my wrist and pulls me towards the bathroom.

'Wait, Dom, what's going on? Where's Andre? Is it over?' My dad pops his head out of the room just as Dom is about to close the bathroom door.

'Andre told me to tell you to sit tight, that he'll be back soon and fill you in on everything.' He doesn't wait for a response and closes the door, locking it before turning around and stripping out of his clothes. I switch the water on, letting it run over my hand to find the perfect temperature before hitting the shower on. He climbs right in and I quickly strip my clothes off and join him. The way he cut my dad off, I get the vibe he's not in the mood for talking. I pull the bath sponge down off the shower shelf and lather it up before beginning to wash him down, starting with his back and working it across his entire body before rinsing the sponge and setting it back on the shelf. He turns and grabs the bar of soap and begins to wash himself all over again, as if he's trying to rid himself of something. I stop his hand, which is vigorously scrubbing at his arm and lace my fingers with his. I pull him into me and hug him close. His body melds against mine and his chest starts to hiccup as he cries. I rub his hair to soothe him, allowing him the time he needs.

CHAPTER TWENTY-SIX

Dom

I FEEL LIKE a pussy as Chloe tiptoes around me, but it's not every day you kill someone in cold blood. The first time it didn't get to me like this, but I didn't have a choice then, it was me or them, I chose me. This time was different I could have walked away I could have left him alive. But after all he's done, and all he threatened to do I couldn't walk away. I couldn't leave him breathing. I had to end it. For all of us. Now all I want to do is get out of this place and go home. See my nan, take Chloe out on a date, be normal. What is normal anymore? Chloe is lying beside me on the bed, stroking my arm in rhythm with her breathing. It's so quiet, Charity and Mike are in the kitchen and its nice. I know she has a million and one questions but she doesn't ask. Instead she gives me exactly what I need without me even asking for it.

'I love you,' I tell her making her look up at me. A small smile creeps across her face and her hand caresses my cheek.

'I love you right back,' she says kissing my lips in a chaste kiss. As she moves to pull back I clasp my hands either side of her face and pull her toward me. She straddles me and crawls up my body, the kiss intensifies and a second later I'm pulling her top up and over her head. Her hands are wandering all over me like she's just as desperate for me as I am for her. I arch my back and she tugs at my t-shirt. I release my arms so she can pull it off. It gets stuck and she giggles as she attempts to free me from it. But as my fingers find her breasts through her bra her serious side returns and her eyes close as I pluck at the nipple beneath the material. I straighten her back and graze the other with my teeth. She sucks in a breath which sounds like a hiss. I look up as her lips form the perfect O, the sight is perfection. I make quick work of her bra and panties and she releases me from my shorts. I get another perfect vision before me as she reaches between us and lowers herself on my dick. God I could be inside this woman forever and it wouldn't get old. As the walls of her pussy grip me tight she moves, riding me with the confidence, like she's done it a million times before. I'm about to take over when there's a knock on the door. Chloe stops dead and I see panic in her eyes as she realises someone might just walk in.

'We'll be out in a little bit.' I shout holding her hips so she can't pull off of me. This is way to fucking good not to finish. And they can fucking wait.

'Chloe, I just wanted a word?' Mike says through the door like he's going to get a different answer than the one I just gave him. I put my finger over Chloe's lips and grin telling her to be quiet.

'She's in the shower right now,' I yell back.

'Oh okay, if you can tell her then?'

'Sure.' Chloe sniggers as I grind my hips up against her pushing myself deeper as her father walks away.

'Oh my god.' She giggles and it does things to the snug little walls surrounding my dick. I groan at the feeling. Rolling her hips, she takes control once again, and I hold onto her hips while she rides the fuck out of me. Her head goes back and her back arches giving me access to her swollen clit, licking my fingers I rub in small circles and that's all it takes for her orgasm to come rolling in. I can feel the second it starts, her thighs clamp around mine and she curves her body toward me her face in the crook of my neck.

'Oh... yes... yes... don't stop,' she whispers, only adding fuel to my fire. I thrust inside her while I torment her clit faster, going harder still until she screams out and I spill myself inside her.

'You are so fucking perfect,' I tell her while she pants collapsing on top of me. We both breathe heavily and we stay like that for a few minutes more. Then reality of what I just did sets in.

'Umm, I didn't use protection.'

'Yeah... About that,' she begins 'I think it's maybe possible... that... I could be pregnant.' My eyes widen as I stare at her in utter shock.

'What?' So far as I know we've been careful 'Are you sure?'

'No... but I haven't had my period and I've been sick, like a lot.'

I sit us up and look her in the eyes. 'So, its a maybe?' she nods but looks down away from me shyly.

'And are you okay with that?'

She shrugs. 'Yeah I think so.' She half smiles. 'Are you?'

'Fuck, I've not even thought about it, but yeah if you are, I guess… we might be parents soon huh?' I grin. Capturing her face, I kiss her slowly and with everything I have.

Pulling back, she smiles. 'So you're really okay with it?'

'Fuck yeah, your belly swollen with my baby, I can't fucking wait!'

***
Chloe

This morning I woke wrapped in Dom's arms. My favourite place to be. I fell asleep last night with a smile on my face, knowing that if the results come back that I am pregnant that'd he'd be happy about it. It felt like a weight had lifted off my shoulders that I didn't even know was there. I heard Andre come in sometime in the middle of the night, but he didn't come to the room so I just assumed everything was okay for now. Dom needed a good night's sleep after all he'd been through. Granted I don't know exactly what that is, but with how much he was torn up, I know it was big.

Dom groans and pulls me in tighter to his body. 'Good morning, baby.' He places a kiss on my head, his morning wood pressing into my back side. But I know now isn't the time, we need to talk to Andre and see what's going on.

'Honey, I think I heard Andre come in sometime last night. Do you think we should go talk to him, see what's going on?' His arm raises off of me and his legs untangle from mine as he pulls himself up to the side of the bed.

'Yeah, I guess we should. Listen no matter what happens out there, Chloe, I just want you to know that I love you with everything that I am.' He turns and gives me a brief kiss before getting up and throwing his clothes on. What was that supposed to mean? Is there no hope of ever finding Patrick?

'I love you too, Dom.' Is all I can think to reply before climbing from the bed myself and putting on my dirty clothes from yesterday. He pulls my hand into his and leads the way out of the room into the kitchen. Surprisingly everyone is already awake and sitting at the table, with mugs of steaming coffee in front of them. Charity is nestled on my dad's lap once again. Right now though, I need to pick my battles and that isn't the top of my priorities.

'Morning,' I mumble as I make my way over to the coffee maker and pour Dom and I cups of coffee, his black, mine with a little cream and sugar. 'So what's the update Andre? Is your man okay?'

'Yes and no. I've come with an update and no Pete didn't make it.' His eyes turn hard as he says it and I know for sure that's his coping mechanism.

'Oh no. I'm so sorry, Andre.' I go over and give him an awkward one arm hug before joining Dom at the breakfast bar. 'What's the update, Andre?' I know it came off as kind of demanding, but I can't help it. I'm so done with all of this.

'He's dead.' Is all he says. I don't know if everyone else is just as confused as I am right now.

'Yeah, you just said, and I truly am sorry for your loss.'

'Not Pete. Patrick. I put three bullets into him last night.' There's a collective gasp around the kitchen from all of us except Dom who just sits there staring down at his hands.

'So he's gone? It's all over now? We don't have to worry about that piece of shit anymore?' As soon as the words come out, I beg to the lord that I could take them back. I look over to Charity and it's as bad as I thought it would be. Her body is shaking and she's crying. I can tell she's trying to hold it in, but the hurt overcomes her. 'I'm so sorry I said that Charity. I know you still loved him no matter what he did. Just as I still love my dad no matter all the crazy things we've been through. I'm so sorry.' I try to backtrack the best I can but it doesn't help any. My dad pulls her tight and cradles her to him, trying to soothe her the best he can.

'We don't need to hear the details, Andre. You can just leave all that out. I think it's for the best that way.' And for once I agree with my dad.

'What will you do now?' I direct my question to Andre.

'You guys get to go back to your lives and I get to go back to Greg. I'm sure I'll have another assignment before I know it. Spending my free time with him, helps to keep me sane.'

'I would love to meet him!' I throw Andre a wink before the weight of his words sets in. 'Go back to our lives.' Geez, I don't even think I know what that is. I glance over to Dom, who still hasn't spoken since we came in here. Maybe it's just the shock of everything being done with? And the shock of a baby that could be on the way and asking me to marry him? Poor Dom, that's a lot to take in.

'Chloe, I know this is a lot to ask but do you think Charity and I can stay at your place while we figure out what our next steps are.' My dad's eyes meet mine.

'Yeah the keys are under the welcome mat. I'll be with Dom. I'm sure Nan is more than ready to get back home.' I hop down from the stool.

'Thank you Chloe I really appreciate that'

'Okay, let's do this. It's time to go home!'

CHAPTER TWENTY-SEVEN

Dom

WE PULL INTO the car park and I look over at Chloe, 'So are we going to do this?' I honestly think I might be a little disappointed if the test shows she's not pregnant, but until we actually get a test we won't know for sure.

'Yep, let's go.' She smiles opening her door and we make our way to the pharmacy and ask the clerk for directions to find what we're looking for. The lady gets up from her stool behind the desk and walks a short way down the aisle, we follow behind,

'They're all here.' She waves her hands indicating a whole section. Chloe looks at me and I at her and back to the huge array of pregnancy tests. How the hell do you choose?

'Umm can you tell me which is the most accurate?' I ask.

The lady thinks on it a second and then she points a small section out. 'This one is the earliest detector, but it's the most expensive. It will tell you in words pregnant or not pregnant, you don't have to worry about lines or whatever. This is the biggest seller too. Easier to determine the result'

'Great Thank-you, we'll take that one?' I look to Chloe for confirmation. Who nods shyly biting her lip. We pick up some groceries and head home.

***

As I pull up outside of the house I sudden sense of sadness seems to settle over us both. I look toward the house next door, where Zoe lives, lived. I still haven't accepted that she's gone. I know she was killed in my house but Chloe doesn't know the details and I'm planning to keep it that way. No need to give her those nightmares too.

We drop the groceries on the counter and head straight for the bathroom, despite me wanting to be there for the actual test, Chloe insists I stand outside because she isn't peeing on a stick in front of me. I chuckle and she swears she will bring it straight out and we will wait for the result together. A few minutes later she opens the door with it in hand. We sit with our backs against the wall of the bathroom with the test upside down. I'm counting the seconds down and Chloe's fingers are tapping an impatient tune out on her knee.

'It's time.' Biting her lip, she turns the test over. The words in the digital square read 'Pregnant.' We look at each other and a smile spreads across my face.

'I'm really pregnant,' she whispers her excitement clear. I grin back at her as she breaks out in a giggle.

'We need to get you a doctor's appointment and make sure everything is okay.'

'I'll call first thing in the morning,' she tells me.

'We also need to get all your stuff from your place and move you in properly.'

'Are you sure you don't need some time with Nan first?'

'Are you kidding me? You want to move in here, right?'

'Of course I do, but I don't want to impose on your nan you know, after all the trouble I've been'

'Hey, not one more word like that, you're my girl and in there.' I caress her stomach. 'Is my baby, you can't be living somewhere else, I'd hate that, and my nan loves you.'

'You're sure about this?'

'Abso-fucking-lutely.' I lift her from her sitting position and pull her up into my arms. 'Now I'm going to feed my pregnant fiancé and then we're going to go and see if Nan wants to come home'

'Sounds perfect.' While I'm standing at the stove throwing ingredients into the wok, she comes up behind me and wraps her arms around my waist.

'What will we do now?'

'What do you mean?'

'Well I had a job and you... Well the fighting? It feels like a lifetime ago.'

'We'll figure it out, let's not dwell on all that right now.'

Nodding her head she agrees. 'Okay.' She looks into the pan. 'Smells so good.'

'Well I'm not promising perfection but I do cook a mean stir fry.' I grin as she giggles at my wagging eyebrows.

'Sit I'll bring it over.' I watch her ass as she walks away and I chuckle as she catches me over her shoulder. I dish up two plates and pour us some juice from the fridge. Then we sit and have our first proper meal together at home in *our* home. It feels right. When we're done we hop back in the car and head out to see Nan. I'm so excited, but more than that, at the same time I'm nervous as hell because without seeing her everyday she may have forgotten who I am completely. Just like she did in the hospital. That possibility has played on my mind the whole time I've been away from her. We get to the desk and the receptionist has us sign in and tells us where we need to go to find her.

Chloe grips my hand and pulls me to a stop, 'Dom wait a second.' We stop and she takes both hands in hers as she looks up at me. 'Maybe you should go in alone?'

'No, no it's fine.'

'Dom, I just don't want to confuse her. If I stay outside maybe there's more chance that she'll recognise you.' I kiss her. I can't help it, the fact that she's thinking about this means so much.

'Babe whether my nan recognises me or not I want you to be there it's important to me.'

'You're sure?'

'Yes I'm sure' We stand for a second before I open the door and head into the lounge area we were told Nan would be. I walk in and find her in a group of around seven others knitting while she chats and laughs with everyone. She looks amazing and happy. I have to say I'm shocked at seeing her so happy.

'Hey Nan?' She looks up and instantly I see the recognition flash in her eyes.

'Oh, Dominic you came to see me!'

'Of course I did, Nan you can't keep me away.'

'Oh, Edna come meet my grandson, isn't he handsome? Oh hello, dear I didn't see you there how are you, Chloe?' Chloe hugs Nan as Edna comes and checks out how handsome I am. I catch Chloe's eye as she steps back from the hug and the smile she's wearing brightens her whole face. We chat for a while with the group while my Nan embarrasses me and tells them all I used to run around naked whenever I had the opportunity as a kid.

When visiting time is almost done, she tells me that we need to go and see her room. We get there and the room is lovely. It's a single so she doesn't have to share and she has everything she needs in there. At one side is a small living area with a TV and comfy chair. She has an electric bed like the kind you get in the hospital and an ensuite. All her personal things are spread around and the place looks so cosy.

'Nan are you ready to come home? I was thinking we could get you packed up tomorrow?'

'Oh, Dom, I've thought about it, and I think I'll be better staying here.' Chloe's just as shocked as I am by the declaration.

'But, Nan, we have your room and Chloe and I would be there for you.'

'Dom, I think you've done enough for me sweetheart, I love you so much, but here is where I should be.'

'Nan it's not about what I've done for you. You have a house you wanted to stay in, I promised you that no matter what you could.'

'I remember.' She cups my face as I kneel in front of her. 'But I didn't know staying in a home would be as nice as this. I have met so many lovely people, Dominic, I really like it here.'

'But the house?'

'It's yours, Dom I signed the paperwork you're a joint owner.'

'What? How... When?'

'When I had to see the solicitor about what your father did. The house is yours now, Dom.'

'But the mortgage?'

'Everything is in your name too, Dom, I knew when I did it that one day I would need care, so this way they can't take the house as payment.' I'm speechless I just don't know what to say.

'So, Nan let me be clear, what you're saying is the paperwork for the house is in both yours and Dom's name?' Chloe asks, and my nan nods.

'The paperwork is all in the cabinet in the dining room.'

I sit down on the floor by her. 'Nan, I can't believe you did that.'

'Why? You would have gotten it anyway. This way you can do whatever you like with it, before I die you don't have to wait.'

'NAN!'

'Oh stop it's going to happen, just know that I'm happy and so very proud of you!'

'Nan, I can't believe you didn't tell me before now.'

'Well it wasn't important before now.'

'I guess' I shrug.

'But, Nan we would like you to come home regardless.'

'Dominic, you have Chloe now you don't need to be worrying about me, my love. I really like it here, and I want you to have your own life. I don't want to be a burden on you, just be sure to visit me!' I look at Chloe for help. What the fuck do I do in this situation?

'Nan you brought me up, you did everything for me, this isn't about you being a burden, I want to have you home.'

'Well I want to stay here so when you visit you need to tell me about your day. Now what time is it because I think we have bingo tonight I don't want to miss it.' And just like that she dismisses the whole fucking thing. We say our goodbyes and as we walk out to the car Chloe looks at me.

'Maybe she'll feel differently tomorrow, we should ask her again then.'

'I doubt it she's never been that lucid for that long since I can remember. That was my nan at her best, Chloe. She was with it and meant every word, she isn't coming home.'

***

Chloe

It's been two weeks since we've found out that we're pregnant and Dom has been a doting fiancé. Quite possibly even a little too much doting. One day when we were making a trip to my apartment, he went all caveman just because I was about to pick up a box.

'Don't you dare, Chloe.'

'It's only a small box.'

'Woman, I don't care what size box it is, I'll get it.' Some days it's nice to have him waiting on me but others, like that one, I may have had the urge to kick him in the shin. Not going to lie, no matter how much he drives me nuts, I love him more and more each day.

It took some sweet talking on Dom's part, but he was finally able to get us an appointment with the gyno. We had to wait two weeks, but that's so much better than the three-month waiting list that they had. We pull up to the office building and before I even have time to unbuckle my seatbelt, Dom is at my door opening it and extending his hand to help me out. Swoon. We make our way up to the fourth floor and down the hall that's labelled Dr. Donna Peters, MD. He opens the door and we both slip in and check in at the receptionist. I feel like we'd been waiting forever by the time a nurse pops her head out of the door and calls my name. I step up on the scale and my weight and height are taken.

'Do you mind peeing in the cup for me? It's just to test some levels that we're able to find in your urine.'

'Sure.' I respond before taking the plastic cup and making my way to the restroom she indicated around the corner. I fill the cup, cap it, and deliver it back to the nurse before being escorted to the exam room. Dom's silent through the whole process and I don't know if it's nerves that are getting to him. I know my nerves are going crazy right now too. I undress and put the gown on, hopping onto the exam table afterwards. Dom comes and stands next to me while we wait for the doctor to join us. There's a few machines around me and I spend the time inspecting them, trying to see if I can figure out what they do.

'How's, mummy doing today?' The doctor asks as she walks into the room and goes to the sink to wash her hands.

'I'm doing alright. A little nervous, but alright.' I start to twist the robe around my fingers.

'No need to be nervous. Today we are just going make sure everything looks alright in there. Dad are you remaining in the room for the examination?' she asks Dom and he stiffens in a 'the fuck I'm going anywhere stance.'

'I'm staying,' is all he replies before going to the other side of the bed to give the Doc some space. He pulls my hand into his and squeezes tight.

The doctor smiles, a long wand is in her hand that looks like it's wearing a condom. Where the hell is she putting that? 'Now if I could have you lay down and scoot your rear to the bottom of the table, I can make sure it all looks well and dandy in there.' I do as she asks and she pushes my legs apart a bit before inserting the probey type thing into my vagina. I've never felt so uncomfortable in my life. But everything else ceases to exist when I look at the monitor and see my little bean.

'Oh my god, Dom.' His hand clenches mine and I feel something wet hit my shoulder. I look up at him and see the brightest smile on his face that I've ever seen and tears slowly trickling down his cheeks. He sees me looking at him and his mouth immediately connects to mine, all the happiness and joy radiating through our kiss.

'I can't wait to make you Mrs Colton.'

EPILOGUE

Dom
18 months later

I FINISH UP at the gym, I can't wait to get home to Chloe and Chase. He's ten months now and already starting to walk, I'm terrified I'll miss his first steps each day I'm not at home. I can't complain though, not many people can say they get paid to keep fit. I started out working there, training people for a wage. Helping with the classes and cleaning the gym at the end of the day, I got to train for free too. I had my first legit MMA fight only a few months after starting there. Now I have sponsors and eight wins under my belt with six being knockouts. When the scouts came to my fight, it was a close one, we went seven rounds and traded blows, until the knock out, I wasn't even sure who was up on points. I was absolutely blown away when I was offered a contract, and even more blown away when they said I'd be paid for it. We get to travel all over with all expenses paid. And I love my job! Turns out that Chloe is a natural when it comes to parenting, she never loses her patience and always has time for Chase even when she's had no sleep. My woman rocks. My phone rings as I step out of the gym.

'Hey, baby everything okay?'

'Hey, everything's great, but we're out of milk and…' she lowers her voice to a whisper. 'My dad just dropped by, he isn't doing so good.'

'Aw shit, okay I'll grab some milk, anything else while I'm there?'

'No I think that's it.'
'Okay see you soon.'
'Oh wait, did you call the home? Check on Nan?'
'I did, she's good.' I smile. She's always thinking about others.
'Oh good I haven't had a second today. That boy is definitely your son.' She giggles,
'Yeah yeah.' I chuckle. 'He just likes to keep mummy on her toes. Babe I'm at the car so if you need anything else text me.'
'Okay love you.'
'Love you, sweetheart be back real soon.'

I sit a while at the junction and think about what I'm walking into when I get home. Chloe and her dad had a long overdue chat just after Chase was born. He and Charity had been deciding whether they should stay in the UK or go back to the States. But Chase being born was the deciding factor. He couldn't leave, and despite Chloe not approving of Charity's relationship with her dad they'd managed to move past it. But Mike had other worries and recently decided that he wanted Charity to go and live a little so she could decide if he was what she really wanted. I think Chloe's words must have penetrated somewhere deep and it bothered him ever since. I mean she did scream about Stockholm syndrome. Charity had argued and argued but he'd insisted. So right now, she's in the States and he's here lonely and feeling very sorry for himself.

It's hard sometimes because I want to tell him to live a little too, not obsess over what Charity's doing. But I understand how hard it must be. He wants her to be sure about him if she does decide to come back. He told her she has to take at least six months or something like that. And in the meantime, he comes over to our house each day and spends time with his daughter and grandson.

Charity's been gone almost three months now. Chloe was reluctant about Mike spending so much time at ours at first, but she's happy with how their relationship stands now and he's even giving her away at the wedding. Which is in two weeks. Wow two weeks and I'll have a Mrs Colton by my side. I can't fucking wait. I pull into the carpark and head into the store. Grabbing some milk, and chocolate because being four months pregnant is messing with Chloe's eating, she craves chocolate like twenty-four hours a day. She's constantly worrying about the weight she's going to gain. But I couldn't care less, being pregnant suits her and honestly, I'd keep her knocked up if it was up to me, she's so fucking beautiful with my babies in her belly. And Chase is so amazing because his mum is. He learns so fast and that along with Chloe's patience in teaching him is just the best thing in the world. I'd have ten kids running around if she'd let me. And honestly we'd have amazing sex making them!

***
Wedding day

I stand at the altar with Andre next to me. He and I have become close after everything, we train together and when he isn't off on a mission he's often round at our house with Greg. They love Chase and we made them his Godfather's. They're amazing, even talked about having their own kids one day. I'm nervous as fuck especially now since Chloe is late. This whole shebang was organised by Chloe and despite having a ten month old and being four months pregnant she's managed to arrange the most beautiful wedding. Not being religious we didn't want a church wedding. But she still wanted to walk down an aisle. So, we chose a hotel which is beautiful and the room has a makeshift altar and an aisle between two sets of seats. Which are filled with our family and friends. And even a kiddie's section with a colouring table for the parents with young children. Chloe thought of everything. The ride here was a surprise too, she had arranged a Ferrari for me and Andre to arrive in. My dream car, and I got to drive it like I was like a kid at Christmas. Chloe has her friend from her old job and her teenage daughter as bridesmaids. I hear the music start and turn back to look I suddenly feel stiff and unable to move. I crack my neck side to side and shake my arms out like I would before a fight. I didn't realise how nervous I was until this very moment.

'Relax, man, it's all good.' Andre winks at me. I smile and his face splits into a grin as he slaps my back. I hear a collective gasp from the guests and I know she must have just walked in. Shit am I supposed to turn around and watch her walk down? Or am I supposed to wait until she's next to me to see her? Is it bad luck if I get it wrong? I look over at Andre who turns and smiles. Fuck it, I can't wait a second longer. I turn my head and catch a glimpse of her. I almost drop to my knees, the image of her in that dress… Jesus I think I'm hard. Fuck I definitely am. I drop my hands to hide the bulge at my crotch and I can't contain the grin that splits across my face.

The dress is white and just off the shoulder, cut in around her tits and showing them in the just best way. Her small bump is just showing under the satin which flows out at her feet and trails behind her in a long sweeping piece that her two bridesmaids are holding a little ways back. The veil sweeps back over her hair but I can see that it is up and curled into ringlets which have little crystals all throughout it.

As always, she's smiling and her eyes are shimmering with brimming tears. As her dad proudly walks her toward me, I feel like I want to meet her half way, but I stand firm and wait. It seems to take forever until her hand is finally in mine.

'Hey,' she whispers.

'Hey, yourself.' I grin. 'You okay?' Her head nods and she bites her bottom lip as the officiant starts to talk. It's all a bit of a blur after that. Until he says, 'You may now kiss the bride.' I don't fucking hesitate and almost drag her off like a caveman to our hotel room there and then. Andre clears his throat and everyone laughs at how desperate I am to kiss her. I don't want to let her go either once I have her in my arms. But a little voice saying, 'Daaeee,' has me turning to find Chase in Andre's arms. There are flashes going off in every corner of the room and by the time we get to the reception room my face hurts from smiling. I look down at our joined hands. Her wedding band is white gold set with diamonds encrusted all the way around. Next to her engagement ring which I chose myself. A square cut diamond sitting in an encrusted band. I take a mental picture. This is one of the best days ever. My wedding band is platinum and plain. I wasn't going to have one at first, fighting isn't the best career to wear a ring. But I know it was important for her just like it was for me to put a ring on her finger. I wouldn't deny her that. I will wear it every day unless I'm in the cage.

The photographer takes a million and one pictures and the final posed ones are us standing by the enormous cake. Which has three tiers and a ton of cupcakes with all different frostings, including my favourite chocolate. My girl did so fucking good with all of this. By the time everyone filters in we're about ready for speeches and food. We sit at the top table and Andre and Greg sit by my nan who occupies the seat next to me. She's still crying with happy tears, and thankfully very lucid. And then Chloe and her dad sit at my other side with Chase in his highchair playing with his teething toys. He looks fucking adorable in his little grey suit and bow tie. With everyone I love surrounding me I couldn't ask for a better day.

'Speech,' someone shouts. I guess I should go first. I stand and clink my glass with a knife.

'I just want to say a few words.' I swallow and realise I have a small lump in my throat. I look down at my wife who looks right back as if I am the best man in the whole world.

'I never knew I wanted to get married, or even settle down, I didn't even realise I was looking for a relationship, until the day Chloe walked into my life. It was always crazy to me the thought of love at first sight, but now I know it's real. Because the day I first saw you, Chloe my life changed forever in the best way. You complete me and make me whole, and who I'm meant to be. You made me a husband, a father and a better man. I will love you always. You are my forever, my lobster as you say.' The tears fall but she giggles at my last words because that's what she's said to me ever-since we saw it on a documentary. Everyone claps at my speech but all I see is my wife. I lean down and kiss her. The rest of the day goes by without a hitch and as the evening wears on Mike takes Chase to our house and babysits for the evening while we stay at the hotel. We still have a little one gate-crashing our hotel suite but we can't send that one off for the night just yet. As I lift her into my arms to carry her over the threshold. She laughs loud calling me silly because obviously this isn't where we live, but I intend on doing everything traditionally. I walk her straight over to the bed and lay her out on it. I part her legs and crawl under the mountain of underskirts until I find her panties. What I find there though makes me pause. She has on a garter and suspenders and stockings. I pull back and ruffling the dress beneath me, I finally find her face.

She's grinning from ear to ear. 'You like?' she asks. This I have to see in its entirety. She knows I have a thing for suspenders and stockings and fuck me does she look good in them.

'Stand up.' I order her as I pull her up to standing. She turns looking over her shoulder presenting me with her ass and the back of the dress which I unclip and unthread the ribbon from their loops, it seems to take forever as I finally get the last loop undone. I slide the dress from her shoulders and down until it gathers at her waist and small bump. I leave the white bra in place and turn her to face me. Her face is full of hunger her arousal just as desperate as mine. Sliding her hands under the dress she pushes it over her hips and it falls into a heap at her feet. The suspender belt sits just below her bump and the white sheer lace leaves nothing to the imagination as she steps out I rove my eyes all the way from her face down to her stocking covered legs and white satin heels. What a fucking image.

'You've spoiled me.' I growl as I put my hands on her hips and pull her in for a kiss.

'Anything for you, husband,' she whispers and my dick jerks in response.

'You're so fucking beautiful, Chloe.'

'Oh god Fuck me, Dom,' she begs. No doubt due to the sex ban she put us on for four days leading up to the wedding day. I honestly don't know where to start. So, I devour her mouth and move down her body with my tongue.

'I swear if you weren't already pregnant, you would have been by the end of tonight,' I tell her through frantic kissing and licking.

'Oh my god that feels so good.' She moans as I slide my fingers inside past her panties and rub on her clit. I pull down her knickers slowly and deliberately grazing my fingers down the inside of her thighs and walk her backward to the bed.

'Lay down, baby.' We spend the whole night making each other come. Before we finally fall asleep exhausted and more than sated.

As the sun comes up I feel her lips on my chest her teeth grazing my nipple, and her hand on my dick.

'Good morning, wife.'

I'm greeted with a grin as she takes my dick inside her mouth. Good fucking morning indeed.

The End

ABOUT THE AUTHORS

Harper and Eva had a chance meeting one day in the book world! Harper needed advanced readers and Eva loved to read. It was a match made in heaven. The two quickly became fast friends, and then became an inseparable duo, author and PA. Just like Thelma and Louise they wanted to conquer the book world! One day they had a conversation about a great story. Harper realised she had a cover that would fit the story perfectly, so the duo began on their second amazing journey together, and Fighting For Chloe was born. Nothing could hold them back as the words started to flow and as each chapter was written it only got more and more exciting!

We can only hope that the enjoyment we found in writing this book will transfer to the readers who took a chance on us.

If you enjoyed our book please leave a review!

And if you would like to find us our links are below:

FOLLOW HARPER PHOENIX:

Amazon ~ https://www.amazon.co.uk/-/e/B01N6MENFY
Newsletter ~ http://eepurl.com/cXsxs1
Goodreads ~ https://www.goodreads.com/book/show/33650901
BookBub ~ https://www.bookbub.com/authors/harper-phoenix
FB Author Page ~ https://m.facebook.com/HarperPhoenix16/
FB Readers Group: Harper's Stone Pack
~ https://www.facebook.com/groups/241659016258029/
Instagram ~ https://www.instagram.com/harper.phoenix
Twitter ~ https://twitter.com/HarperPhoenix1

FOLLOW EVA JONES:

HARPER PHOENIX, EVA JONES

Newsletter ~ http://eepurl.com/dGA0ff
Goodreads ~
https://www.goodreads.com/author/show/17743130.Eva_Jones
FB Author Page ~
https://www.facebook.com/authorevajones/
FB Multi-Author Group: Sassy Classy Bad Assy Bitches ~
https://www.facebook.com/groups/1976910769204413/
Instagram ~
https://www.instagram.com/evajonesauthor/
Twitter ~ https://twitter.com/EvaJone44428870

Made in the USA
Columbia, SC
02 March 2019